PORNSTAR

CLUB RADIANT

EMILIA ROSE

CHAPTER
ONE

ATHENA

"NO," I mumbled to myself, pacing around in our kitchen and shaking my head. The mahogany hardwood was cold underneath my feet, and the low hum of our central heat did nothing to calm my racing heart. I crossed my arms over my chest to hide my taut nipples. "It can't be Charlie. I … I can't believe it."

No way was my best friend an adult entertainer.

Heat swelled in my core, and I gripped the kitchen island until my knuckles turned white. He was the definition of puppy dog with big blue eyes—the nicest, sweetest man I had ever met. He'd help me with anything I asked, and he wasn't one of those rich snobs just because he had come from a wealthy East Coast family.

I squeezed my eyes closed, replaying the moment last night when I had realized that the man I had been gawking at for months now was not only my best friend, but also my roommate.

What was I thinking?!

When I recognized his room in the background, I should've closed the tab immediately. But instead, I rewatched every single one of his videos to make sure that it was really him. Charlie never showed his face, but I knew his body too well. Those tattoos and his scar.

I even paid him to grunt and growl my name last night because I wanted to hear it so badly. He had said my name many times before in person, so softly spoken, but last night, it had been fucking wild, rowdy.

"Morning." Charlie yawned from the doorway with his sun-kissed skin, light blonde almost-white hair, and sculpted muscles taunting me.

After leaping up in surprise, I twirled around and backed up into the counter. He rubbed his eyes the way he did every morning when he woke up, tired from staying up all night.

"Morning," I squeaked and hurried past him.

"What's wrong?" he asked almost immediately, catching my wrist before I could escape.

When he turned me around, another squeal left my mouth. I held my hands over my chest to hide my aching nipples and attempted to come up with an excuse. Any excuse. Something that would be believable at the very least!

"Um … nothing. Why?"

His gaze dropped down to my hand-covered chest, and then he lifted it back up to mine, his jaw twitching. God, he was screaming all kinds of trouble this morning!

He gently tightened his grip on my wrist. "What's wrong, Athena?"

I needed to get out of here. Now!

"Nothing!" I exclaimed and hurried toward the door. "Nothing at all."

"Come on, Athie." Before I could make it three feet past him, he wrapped his hand around the nape of my neck and gently tugged me backward against his muscular body. "I know you. You can tell me if something's—"

"I think I forgot something, um …" My gaze snapped around the hall. "In my room!"

After escaping his grasp for good, I sprinted past him and down the hall to my bedroom. What was wrong with me this morning? Why couldn't I get my-damn-self together around him? I had touched myself one too many times to his videos, but I had never reacted like this …

Maybe it was because he'd said my name last night. Or that I now knew it was him.

Once I reached my room, I slammed the door and ran to my computer because my dumb ass had fallen asleep to his videos, and I realized that I had never closed the tabs. I whipped my fingertips along my touchpad to turn it on.

The screen glowed, and my favorite video of Charlie's lit up.

Fuck, what is wrong with me?! Why didn't I close all these tabs?!

"Can I come in?" Charlie asked while opening my bedroom door, his blue eyes huge.

I snapped my laptop shut and stood in front of the computer. "U-um … ye—no."

He walked into the room anyway with a smile so soft that I couldn't believe the man I had watched last night was really him. There was no way in fucking hell that it was him. The man in the video was vicious, dark, filthy-mouthed, and … loved choking.

The Charlie I knew apologized if he accidentally bumped into me.

"Fuck," I whispered, nipples aching.

"What is it, Athena?" he asked, moving closer to me. "Sierra, Heather, and Sun aren't supposed to be over for another hour or so, right? We have time. You can tell me what happened. Why are you acting so weird?"

"I can't," I whispered, heart pounding the closer he came.

"Why not? Did something happen at the bar last night?"

"No."

He grimaced and looked past me at the laptop. "Is it something on your computer?"

"No!"

My quick and rushed response did nothing to convince him. Actually, the opposite happened as he stepped past me and grabbed the laptop from behind my back. "I swear, if someone is harassing—"

"Wait! Don't open th—"

Before I could reach for it, he opened my laptop. The video of him pounding his cock into another woman's throat, slapping her tits, and spitting on her face began playing on full blast because my earbuds weren't connected anymore and I hadn't gotten a chance to close all the damn tabs!

"It's not what it looks like!" I shrieked, slamming the laptop shut. "I'm sorry! I'm so sorry!"

We were best fucking friends, and I had been touching myself to him, thinking about how it'd feel if I were the one he was face-fucking like that. It was *exactly* how it looked, and I felt so guilty for it.

I turned my head and averted my gaze, my chest and face suddenly burning. "I'm so sorry. I found it online, and I ... I knew it was you. You have the same tattoos, the same scar on your finger. And I ..."

Oh God! This was going to ruin our entire friendship!

Seven years down the drain.

Suddenly, he wrapped his hand around my throat and pinned me to the nearest wall. I sucked in a breath and stared up into his dark eyes, my heart pounding inside my chest and my pussy clenching.

"You what?" he growled. "Found out it was me and decided to touch yourself to it?"

While I opened my mouth to protest, only a whimper escaped my throat.

A low, deep chuckle rumbled from his body, and then he drew the pad of his thumb across my lower lip. The submissive in me sucked in another breath and stared up at him, waiting, anticipating his next move.

"If you wanted me to treat you like a dirty little fuckdoll all this time, you could've said so," he said, slipping his thumb between my lips and watching as I sucked on it. He cursed under his breath, his gaze hazy.

"I'm sorry," I whispered, sucking on it harder. "I'm sorry. I couldn't stop myself."

"Fucking hell," he snarled, shoving me to my feet.

I landed on my knees, my pussy aching and desperate, and I stared up at him through wide eyes. He reached down and pinched my hardened nipples through my tank top, tugging them as hard as he could.

"It was you last night who paid me to moan your name, wasn't it?"

"N-no."

He pulled on my nipples harder. "Don't fucking lie to me."

"Yes, it was," I cried. "It was me!"

He released my tits and slid his hands up to my jaw, shoving his fingers into my mouth to wet them, drawing them all across my face, lightly tapping my cheek, as if to test what I really liked, how far I really wanted to go with him.

"That's what I thought. Now be a good girl for me and open your mouth."

CHAPTER
TWO

ATHENA

WHEN I OBEYED my best friend's demand, Charlie shoved four fingers back into me and toward the back of my throat, making me gag on him. He wiggled them around, testing me, *preparing* me for his huge cock.

"Are you going to be a good girl for Daddy?" he hummed, thrusting his fingers in and out of my throat.

Spit and drool rolled down my chin and onto my tank top, which barely even hid my small tits anymore.

"Mmhmm," I said, drooling and choking on his fingers.

"What was that?"

"Mmhmm!"

He grabbed a fistful of my hair at the top of my head and bobbed it back and forth, forcing me to choke myself on his fingers. "Nodding for me, sweetheart." He pounded them faster into my mouth. "Keep going, baby. Get that throat ready for me."

When he finally pulled my head back, I collapsed onto my hands, coughing and spitting up drool. He pulled my head back by my hair and undid the string of his gray sweats with his free hand. My pussy tightened, heat exploding throughout my core.

I grabbed his waistband and yanked his pants down to his ankles as he gripped his huge cock in his hand, pre-cum already dribbling off the head. Another wave of pleasure rushed through me, and I pressed my thighs together.

This is wrong, but I can't stop.

Before he could growl another word, I wrapped my hands around the base and pulled him closer, moving my mouth around his dick and dragging my tongue across his head, thrusting him inside me.

"I've been waiting to fuck you like this for years," he grunted. "Fucking years, Athie."

After I slowly took him inside me twice, he tightened his grip on my hair so I couldn't move and then pounded himself deep into my throat. I choked and gagged on him, but he refused to stop and even went so far as to thrust himself deep enough so my lips were pressed against his pelvis as he pinched my nose closed.

I placed my hands on his thighs, air restricted, and attempted to pull back.

But again, he refused to let me move.

"Touch yourself," he growled. "Rub that aching pussy for me."

Through teary eyes, I stared up at him and thrust a hand between my legs, rubbing my clit in torturous little circles. I opened my mouth wider, both to breathe and to moan, but he plugged me up with his balls.

He wrapped my red hair around my throat and used it to choke me. "Every fucking time I'm with someone else, I imagine it's you that I'm ruining."

I rubbed my pussy faster, the ecstacy exploding through my core. One more moment passed, and then he released his hold on me. I collapsed onto my back, my legs too weak to hold me up as ecstasy rushed through my body.

This was what he probably told all the girls before he started recording, but to me, the words sounded so special. Maybe it was because I had waited for this day for so long, but had been so nervous to make the first move.

"F-fuck!" I cried. "Oh my G-G-God!"

He dropped between my thighs, yanked off my shorts, and thrust his fingers into my aching cunt. I pulsed tightly around him, the pleasure still pumping out of me. I cried out when he drew his fingers in a come-hither motion against my G-spot.

"Spread your legs wider," he ordered.

I spread them wider and watched impatiently as he moved between them, dragging his hands up and down my bare thighs, like he had wanted to touch me like this for so long, like he wanted to *savor* it.

Instead of plunging himself inside me, he rubbed my clit with the head of his dick. I reached toward him and clutched his thighs with my fingers, my pussy tightening even harder.

"Please," I begged. "Please, fuck m—"

Before I could get another word out, he shoved himself into me. My body jerked up into the air, my back arching. I spazzed out around him until he finally leaned forward, placed his forearms on either side of my head, and then kissed me.

When his lips met mine, he slammed himself into me as fast and hard as he could. His kiss was soft, but his thrusts were brutal. I parted my lips, allowing for him to slip his tongue into my mouth, and tightened around him, wanting to blurt out all the feelings I had for him.

But I couldn't get myself to do it.

After all, this was happening because I'd found out his dirty secret. Not because he liked me.

"Where do you want it?" he murmured after ten minutes of orgasm after orgasm.

If I told him that I wanted him to dump his load inside my pussy, he'd laugh right in my face. I had never once seen him come inside anyone's pussy before, only ever on their faces and very rarely down their throats.

"Please, don't stop," I cried instead, dragging my nails down his back. "Please!"

"Where do you fucking want it, you dirty little whore?"

I tightened my pussy around him and pretended like I hadn't heard.

He chuckled darkly. "Your pussy got all tight, Athie. You want it inside you?"

My cheeks flushed, and I tried to hide my face in the crook of his shoulder because I was so embarrassed. There was no doubt in my mind that he would pull out. I was just another girl to him, someone he could get off to, just his friend.

"I'm going to make you fucking say it one way or another, so you'd better start talking."

"Charlie," I whispered.

He smacked my cheek. "Where do you want it?"

No response.

Smack.

"Where do you want it?"

Still nothing.

Smack.

"Where do you fucking wan—"

"Inside me, please!" I cried, unable to stop myself.

My body was doing all kinds of betraying me today. He shouldn't even be inside me right now, so I shouldn't care. But I felt so wrong, so dirty. Charlie was my best friend, my best fucking friend whose cock was now plunged deep into my cunt.

"Please," I cried. Begged. "Please, Charlie!"

His thrusts became even quicker. He wrapped his arms underneath my shoulders and grasped them, pulling me toward him with every thrust. "I've never come inside a woman," he growled, voice husky in my ear.

"I-I know," I cried out, about to explode again. "I'm sorry for asking. Y-you don't ha—"

Before I could finish my sentence, he slammed his cock deep into my pussy and grunted. He stilled for a couple of moments, not pulling out as his dick twitched inside me, and then he shoved his cum even deeper.

"Charlie!" I cried, coming all over him.

Through hazy eyes, he watched me come down from my fifth orgasm of the morning. And only then did he pull out of my pussy, spreading my legs and admiring his cum dripping out of my pulsing hole.

"Charlie," I whispered, sitting up on my forearms.

My heart pounded inside my chest as my gaze dropped to his cum drooling onto the rug underneath us. I went to stand, to wipe it all out of me because this wasn't right. We were best friends.

But he caught me and shoved his fingers into my cunt, pushing his cum back inside me. "Mine," he growled. "This pussy is now mine, Athie."

CHARLIE

ATHIE TIGHTENED AROUND MY FINGERS, her pussy gripping on to me like she didn't want me to pull out, and curled her fingers against my biceps. Her legs started shaking even more violently, and her pretty, full lips parted.

"Ch-Ch-Charlie," she whispered. "I-I'm going to—"

"Athena!" Heather, Athena's friend, shouted from the living room. She must've had a key.

Athena widened her eyes and snatched my wrist. "Shit! Why are they here so—"

Instead of stopping, I continued to curl my finger over her G-spot, massaging it to make my girl feel good. I had been waiting for this moment since I'd met Athie years ago, and I wasn't going to let her leave this room without satisfying her.

"Charlie," she whispered. "You have to stop! They're here!"

I rested my forehead on hers and curled my fingers faster, loving the way that her little pussy gripped me. She pushed at my hand and bit down on her bottom lip, small little whimpers escaping her mouth.

"Athena, where are you?" Heather shouted.

"I'll be out in a … in a minute!" Athena yelled back. "I'm ch-changing!"

"Look at you," I murmured against her lips. "I bet that pressure in your core is too much for my pretty girl." I peppered kisses down her jaw, then down the column of her neck, finding her soft spot. "It's okay. Let it all out, baby," I cooed.

When her entire body arched hard up into me, I pressed my mouth against hers. She moaned softly against my lips, her arms convulsing and her pussy clenching and unclenching around my fingers. I pushed my cum deeper inside her.

She might've been on birth control, but I knew she forgot to take it some days.

And, God, the thought of Athie carrying our child …

"Fuck," I growled into her mouth.

I could never—*ever*—say that aloud to her, but it made me hard again.

Once she finally came down from her orgasm, she lay back on the rug and stared up at the ceiling, her long red hair sprawled all around her. I grabbed my pants, heart pounding inside my chest.

Did that really just … happen?

"Damn, you're taking a long time," Heather said from the hallway, approaching the room.

After quickly tugging up on my pants, I grabbed a basket of laundry that Athena had in the corner of her room and slipped out the door before Heather had a chance to barge in and see Athena naked on the bed.

I bumped into her with the basket of laundry between us. "Sorry, didn't see you there."

"What are you doing in Athena's room?" Heather asked, wiggling her brows at me while Athena's other friends, Sierra and Sun, looked over from the couch in the living room.

"Grabbing her clothes to start a load of laundry," I said,

tilting my head and lifting the basket full of clothes. I flashed her a believable and innocent smile—the same one I had given Athena countless times after I jerked off while streaming, thinking about her.

"Mmhmm," Heather hummed, walking to the kitchen to grab a bowl for the popcorn she had already started popping in the microwave.

Sierra and Sun returned to searching Netflix for movies that they wanted to watch.

I headed past them to the laundry room and shut the door behind me, dumping the basket on the floor and leaning back against the wall. While my dick had been hard a couple of moments ago, it had softened, but the front of my pants was wet from the last few drops of cum.

Fuck, I can't believe what I just did.

Before shoving Athena's clothes into the washer, I found a pair of her pink panties.

They were dirty, but I couldn't get the thought of Athena wearing these last night when she had watched me moan her name and jerk my dick to one of her many pictures that we had taken together over the years.

Would this ruin our friendship? I didn't know. That depended on Athie.

I didn't want to ruin our friendship, but I couldn't control myself after I found out that she had been watching me perform. It hadn't only been one video either. She had several tabs open to my account. She had paid me to moan her name last night.

She was a regular too. I recognized her username.

All this fucking time, if I had known that was how she liked being treated, if I had known that she liked me—even in the slightest way—like that, it would've been her that I was bending over the bed to fuck. I wouldn't have even started porn.

But I had needed a way to get out all my sexual frustration from being around her.

When I walked out of the laundry room, Athena glanced over at me from the couch. Her cheeks flamed a bright red, almost as bright as her hair, and she quickly averted her gaze to the screen, where a movie started playing.

My phone buzzed in my pocket.

Nadia: When are we meeting up next week to film? 😗

Nadia: I've been waiting for so long. xx

I sucked in a sharp breath, glanced back at Athena—who shifted on the couch, a strand of her hair falling into her soft face—and slipped my phone into my pocket without responding.

Nadia and I had been planning to film together for months. Everyone had asked me to film a scene with her, and apparently, her followers were excited to see her get face-fucked too.

But—my stomach turned—*I don't know.*

"You girls want anything while I'm out?" I shouted from the kitchen.

"No," Sierra said.

"No, thanks," Sun said quietly.

"Nah," Heather said.

Athena continued to stare at the screen and swallowed hard. From here, I could tell she wasn't paying attention to the movie at all. She had heard what I said, but decided to ignore me because her friends *always* poked fun at how close we were.

I opened the door. "Athena?"

"I'm good," she said, her voice shaky. *"Full."*

A low, possessive growl escaped my throat, but I slipped out the door before any of the girls could hear it. *Full of my cum.*

She hadn't had a chance to clean herself off before her friends stopped over. She was covered in sex.

After stepping into the elevator, I hit the bottom button for the parking garage. My phone buzzed again in my pocket, and I knew it was Nadia. She was way too needy for my liking, but we had already signed a contract together for this film.

I blew out a low breath and leaned against the back elevator wall. I needed a drink.

And the best place for one of those in Pittsburgh was Club Radiant. Besides, I was sure that Steven and Hector Patton could give me some advice on this sudden change of events that was quickly unfolding.

CHAPTER
FOUR

ATHENA

THREE HOURS AFTER CHARLIE LEFT, we had watched one and a half movies for our weekly girls' day, and I hadn't stopped thinking about everything that had happened this morning.

Was this real life?! What were we? Did he have feeling—

Suddenly, Sierra paused the really bad horror movie we were watching.

"Did something happen with Charlie?" Heather asked, smirking at me.

"No!" I exclaimed, tugging the pillow to my chest. "Why do you think that?"

Thank God my hair is long enough to cover the marks he left on my body!

"You're acting kinda weird," Sierra said.

"Am I?" I asked—definitely suspiciously.

Think, Athena! Come up with some type of an excuse.

"And what are these?!" Heather exclaimed, pushing my hair over my shoulder and staring with wide eyes at the hickeys that Charlie had left all over me.

I'd thought I was way past the age of getting hickeys, but …

Charlie had transformed into a wild animal a couple of hours ago, claiming me in ways that no other man ever had. Deep down, I secretly loved that he had left marks on my body and come inside of me when he never did that to any other girl—at least in his videos.

But it was going to be a bit hard to explain because I didn't want them to think we were something when we weren't.

I wasn't sure what Charlie thought we were after that. Did he still want to be friends? Friends with benefits?

I didn't want to lose him.

"I, um …" I started, my throat closing. "They're from …"

"Charlie?" Sun smirked.

"No!"

"Are you seeing Charlie?!" Heather squealed. "I knew it! We've been—"

"These aren't from Charlie," I said quickly so she wouldn't come up with this entire scenario in her head.

It'd probably meant nothing to him. He slept with so many girls anyway. I was just another one.

"Then who are they from?"

"His brother," I blurted out without thinking about the consequences.

As soon as the words left my mouth, everyone suddenly became quiet. I opened and closed my mouth a handful of times, trying to find a better excuse, but I literally couldn't think of anyone else who'd be acceptable.

Who else could I say?

"Derek?" Sierra asked as the front door opened.

"Did someone say Derek?" Charlie asked, holding cheesecake from my favorite bakery, Doughburgh. He placed the cheesecake on the counter and glanced at me. "Did he stop over?"

"No," I said, turning my gaze away and cursing to myself.

Why the hell did I say Derek and literally not anyone else?!

"Oh." Heather giggled. "Athena was just telling us about last night."

I glared at the side of her head for bringing him up, but this was my fault.

"And my brother came up?" Charlie asked from the kitchen, unboxing the cheesecake.

"Yeah," I mumbled, sinking deeper into the couch. "Somehow."

"Apparently, he came over," Sierra teased, bumping her shoulder with mine.

Fuck! God, Charlie is going to hate me after this!

In the reflection of the TV screen, I spotted Charlie pausing mid-cut. I gulped and hoped that he would drop it and return to his normal bubbly self. I really didn't want him asking any more questions that I couldn't answer.

"Who wants cheesecake?" Charlie asked after a second. When the girls didn't say much, he placed two big slabs on plates, walked over to us, and handed me one. Charlie plopped down beside me. "What are we watching?"

Heather yawned and stood. "We *were* watching this horror thing, but it got kinda boring."

"Anyway, Steven is waiting for me. We're supposed to go to dinner tonight," Sierra said.

I followed them toward the door.

Heather placed her hands on Sun's shoulders and squeezed. "And *someone* has a date tonight with a certain couple at Radiant! I'm going to help her get ready for it. A, you wanna come with us?"

I swallowed hard and looked at Charlie sitting on the couch, his fork sliding into the cheesecake to break off a piece. To anyone else, he looked like the fun, calm, and collected Charlie that everyone loved.

But he was gripping his fork a bit too roughly.

"I'm going to stay here," I said, beaming at Sun. "But have fun. I want all the details!"

Sun blushed and hid her face in Heather's shoulder. "You don't have to tell everyone."

"Yes, I do," Heather said. "This is your first relationship. And with a married couple!"

Sierra giggled. "A married couple?"

"Sun snagged literally the two hottest people who attend Radiant," Heather said.

"I'm jealous," I played along, but it only seemed to make Charlie grip the fork harder.

Heather looped her arm around Sun's and dragged her to the door with Sierra hot on their heels while trying to tug on her winter coat.

"We'll see you later!" Heather called.

Then, the door swung closed.

I sucked in a sharp breath, unsure of what to say to Charlie. Talking about Derek—*insinuating* anything with Derek—really was going to screw me, if it hadn't already.

A moment later, Charlie's arm came around my shoulders, and he plunged his forkful of cheesecake into my mouth, the way he usually did whenever we had some dessert.

"How is it?" he asked, his upbeat self.

Though I could tell that he felt bothered.

I chewed and swallowed. "It's good."

"Want another?"

"No," I whispered, peering back at him. "Are we going to talk about it?"

"Talk about what?" Charlie asked.

"You know," I said, shifting my weight from side to side.

Hell, *I* didn't know whether I was talking about earlier today or Derek anymore.

"Is my cum still buried deep in that pussy?" Charlie hummed.

My entire body suddenly felt like it was in flames. I crossed my arms over my chest and shuffled my feet together, my thighs grinding in the process. "Charlie, I … you …" My nipples hardened underneath my shirt, and then I finally breathed out a, "Y … es."

"Then I don't think we have anything to talk about." Charlie moved closer to me until his hardening cock was pressed against my right hip. He snaked a hand around the front of my throat and pulled me closer until his mouth pressed against my ear. "You're mine. Understand?"

I stared up at his piercing blue eyes and nodded.

He slowly drew his thumb across my lower lip, then popped it into my mouth. "Say it."

"I'm yours," I mumbled against his thumb.

"I own you now, Athie."

Heat rushed to my core, and I pressed my thighs together to suppress the ache between them. "Yes."

"Good girl," he said, gaze shifting from my eyes to my mouth and then back to my eyes. He took off my top, then my bottoms, then continued, "Now get on your knees, open your mouth, and ask Daddy to give you his cock."

CHAPTER
FIVE

ATHENA

WITHOUT HESITATION, I dropped to my knees. I didn't know how he did it, but Charlie had a pull so freaking strong over me that if he asked me to do *anything*, then I probably would without questioning him.

My pussy was gushing in anticipation, and I peered up at him. "Give me your cock."

He reached into his pants and pulled up on his dick so I watched the outline move up and up toward his waistband, until his veiny cock popped out. "So demanding, baby. Ask politely for it."

"Please, can I have it?"

"Where do you want it?"

"Anywhere," I breathed. "I just need you inside me … badly."

Once he laced his fingers into my hair, the heel of his hand on the top of my forehead, he pulled my head back and placed the head of his cock on my lips. When I went to suck it into my mouth, he pulled it back and clicked his tongue.

"Open your mouth and stick your tongue out."

When I did as ordered, he placed his cock on the tip of my tongue.

"So submissive," he noted. "You do everything I say."

"Please."

"Has your pussy been wet all day by you just thinking of me?"

"Yes."

His lips curled into a smirk, and he pushed a couple of inches of his dick into me.

My throat was sore from this morning, and I could barely take half of him in my mouth before choking. I spit up some saliva and looked back up at him, my pussy aching to be filled by his huge cock.

I moved closer to him and sat back on my heels, wrapping my hands around the base of his dick. It was huge, veiny, and thicker than it was on camera.

And, God, I still couldn't believe that this was happening for a second time today.

"No hands," he said. "You don't need help. Please Daddy with your mouth. You can do that, right, Athie?"

Heat exploded in my core when he murmured his nickname for me. I sucked more of him into my mouth and swirled my tongue around his shaft. He curled his fingers into my hair and grunted.

"Look at you," he whispered, gently brushing the fingers of his opposite hand down my cheek. "You're so pretty with my cock in your mouth, with these tears filling your eyes, your cheeks all red."

Fuck. Fuck. Fuck. Fuck. Fuck. Fuck. Fuck.

I sucked more of him into my mouth, desperate to please him. I didn't want him to see me as just another girl he hooked up with. I wanted to be his best, though I knew I was far, far from it. I'd never be able to compare to that girl who didn't have a gag reflex or the brunette with big eyes.

But I could at least try. For him.

When I took more of him into my mouth, I gagged, but didn't stop.

If this didn't work out, we could still be friends. *Hopefully.*

"Rub that pretty little pussy for me," he said.

After dropping a hand between my thighs, I rubbed my clit. With every torturous little circle, the pressure built higher inside my core. I moaned around his cock, tears welling up in my eyes from how deep he was inside me.

"Fuck," he groaned, looking into the mirror. "Your ass is perfect."

A wave of heat coursed through my body. I leaned forward onto my hands, lifted my ass off my heels, and crawled closer to take more of his cock into my mouth and to show him how wet my pussy was for him.

"Look at your pussy drooling for me." He slapped one of my ass cheeks and watched the way it bounced in the mirror.

I might not have tits like most of the girls he hooked up with, but my ass wasn't half bad.

"So fucking sexy. I want to record us so I can jerk off to it later."

My eyes widened, and I clenched hard.

Does he mean, like ... record with him? He ... there's no way. I couldn't ...

He definitely watched my pussy tighten in the mirror because a low chuckle left his mouth as I gagged more on his cock. "Would you like that? Hmm? Show the world how wet your pussy gets for me?"

Fuck! I rubbed my clit harder and nodded.

"Use your words," he commanded.

"Mmhmm," I said, my words muffled by his dick in my throat. "I hanht hit. I hanht hit!"

After cursing underneath his breath, he grunted, "Tell me how long you've wanted *me.*"

I squeezed my eyes closed and hoped that he wouldn't even notice that I didn't answer. I couldn't tell him that I had had a crush on him since the beginning. What if he didn't feel the same? What if he had only wanted to sleep with me?

Chest tightening, I peered up at him through teary eyes and took more of him inside my mouth. I bobbed my head back and forth without using my hands, like he had instructed me, spit and drool rolling off my chin and onto my chest.

When he pulled out of me, I kept my mouth open and my tongue out. "Please, more."

He took his cock in one of his hands and gripped it at its base. "Where do you want it?"

"On my face," I cried, rubbing my clit hard and fast. "Please, come on my face."

While I expected him to run a hand through my hair and move closer to me so he could decorate my face with his cum, he stroked it a few times and stared down at me like he expected a different response.

But he only came on girls' faces.

"I want to come inside your pussy."

My eyes widened as a sudden gush of pleasure rushed to my core. And before I knew it, I was up off my knees and tossed onto the couch by Charlie, like he was some savage animal, ready to claim his next meal.

He climbed between my legs and didn't even think twice about spilling into me because as soon as he slid it in, he was groaning and grunting in a way that I had never heard in any of his videos. Not even the ones with pretty girls.

I curled my fingers around his muscular shoulders and exploded around his huge cock, my back arching and moans escaping my lips. He crawled further up the couch, pushing and pushing himself deeper inside me until his balls pressed up against my aching cunt.

"It's too much," I exclaimed.

Why did he keep pushing it deeper inside me? I didn't know. But the pressure of him driving his hips against my clit continued to push me through the second orgasm of the night.

"You can take it," he murmured, voice gruff. "My girl can take it."

My eyes rolled back, and I curled my toes as another orgasm ripped through my body.

"Oh my God!" I cried, digging my nails deep into his muscular back and clawing down it, surely leaving marks all over his body. But I didn't care.

He had left marks on mine, and whenever he filmed another solo video, everyone would know that he belonged to someone.

Me.

CHAPTER
SIX

CHARLIE

WHEN I WALKED INTO RADIANT—A BDSM club in the heart of Pittsburgh—the scent of vanilla and sex drifted through my nostrils. I had popped in earlier, but nobody that I wanted to talk to was here, so instead, I had opted for Doughburgh's famous cheesecake.

After depositing my coat at the front, I spotted Michelle—one of the owners of Radiant and Hector's sister—walking down the hallway toward the offices, and I headed her way. "Hey, Michelle. Is Hector here?"

"Hate to break it to you, Charles, but Hector is taken," Michelle teased.

"Ah, you got me," I said, playing along. "If you see him, tell him I need to talk to him."

"He should be here later tonight"—Michelle giggled—"but he's out with Heather now."

Damn it.

Well, since I was already here, I might as well wait for him. So, I headed toward the main bar. Girls danced around poles as couples watched on black leather couches. I inhaled the scent of liquor and spotted one of Athena's friends in the crowd.

Sun sat with Russ and Maya, who frequented Radiant, on a couch, sipping on a glass of champagne, her cheeks red with embarrassment. They must've been the couple that Heather had mentioned earlier.

I headed toward the bar and found a seat up front.

"Charlie," Abdul, the bartender, said. "You want your regular?"

I slipped him my black card. "Please."

My phone buzzed in my pocket, and I expected to see Athena's name pop up on the screen. Athena had fallen asleep almost immediately once we finished, and I hadn't wanted to wake her to let her know where I was going.

Besides, I didn't know what I would've said to her anyway.

Truth was, when she had asked me if I wanted to talk about what had happened this morning, I really didn't because I didn't want her to tell me that she just thought of us as friends. That would have fucking crushed me.

But on the other hand, I really didn't know what to do. I didn't know how to label us. Did she even want a label? Just friends? Fuck buddies? She meant more to me than that—she always had—but if she only wanted to be friends, then I would gladly only be friends with her.

It would hurt like a bitch, but I refused to lose her.

As Abdul slid me the drink, I pulled out my phone, thinking about how when I'd left her, my cum had been dripping out of her pussy and staining the couch. I'd get us a new one tomorrow, but I thought it'd be a nice reminder of who she belonged to when she woke up and saw it.

Nadia: Let me know babe. xx

Nadia: Can't wait to finally meet you. 😍

Nadia: We're going to have such a good time. 😏 😏

A low growl escaped my mouth. *Fuck.*

"Thought I'd find you here," Derek suddenly said, squeezing my shoulder.

Double fuck. He was the very last person I wanted to talk to right now.

"What are you doing here?" I asked through gritted teeth.

"Down in the city for a bit. Thought I'd come see you."

"You came to my place yesterday?"

"Pretty girl answered the door," he said. "Athena, was it?"

I sipped on my vodka. So, Heather hadn't been lying or trying to get the best of me when they were over this morning. Athena had been alone yesterday with Derek, and it pissed me off to no end.

For a moment earlier, I'd thought that she had made up some excuse to Heather that Derek had been over last night. Maybe to make me angry, to see how I'd react, or to hide what had really happened this morning.

But Derek had been over, and she hadn't even told me about it.

Though ... I wasn't sure *when* she would have had a chance. As soon as I had found out that she saw my videos this morning, I pounced on her and then left her to her friends. And when I had come home, I couldn't keep my hands off her.

After swishing the vodka in my mouth, I swallowed. "Mmhmm."

"You fucking her?"

"We're friends," I said because I didn't want to turn it into this whole thing. I wasn't sure how Athena felt about me yet. I was too scared to ask and ruin the friendship we had built over the past few years.

"*Just* friends? Huh."

My gaze dropped to my drink, and I swayed the alcohol in the glass. "Just friends."

"You're letting a baddie walk around your house, and you haven't even been tempted to"—a low chuckle came out of my idiot brother's mouth—"you know, sleep with her?" He stretched out on the stool. "If it were me, I would've tapped that the day she moved in."

"I bet you would've," I murmured.

He only cared about a good fuck.

"She's got a nice ass, but her tits need wor—"

"She doesn't need anything," I snarled, glaring at him and hoping that he'd fucking leave already while I figured out what I was going to do—both with Athena and now with Nadia texting me nonstop too. "What do you want anyway? Why are you here?"

"Mom and Dad are hosting a party at the end of January. You coming?"

"No."

"Ah, come on." He slung his arm over my shoulders. "It'll be fun."

"I have work."

He dramatically rolled his eyes. "Work this and work that. It's not like you need the money. Grandpap is about to kick the bucket, and we'll get our inheritance. Why don't you relax for once?"

"Because I like it."

"It's a start-up."

"So what?"

"Damn, it's like talking to a brick wall. Maybe this is why you're in the friend zone." He hopped off the stool and squeezed my shoulder once more. "I'll leave you to wallowing. I'll be in the city for a few days. Think about the party."

After tipping my drink in his direction so I wouldn't have to respond, I placed it back on the counter and slid it to the bartender, watching my brother disappear into the crowd. "Another one."

"She's not just a friend, is she?" Abdul asked.

I stared down at my phone and swiped away Nadia's

messages so I didn't have to look at them any longer. I hoped she'd get the hint and stop messaging me before she came to visit. Hell, I needed to figure out *what* I was going to do—and what Athena and I were—before Nadia stepped on the plane to come here.

"No," I whispered. "She's never been."

CHAPTER
SEVEN

CHARLIE

"HECTOR!" the barista shouted, placing a coffee on the counter of Mug Shot Café.

I lifted my gaze while Hector grabbed his coffee, then returned it to my phone to continue typing out a message to Athena. It was four in the afternoon, which meant that she'd be getting out of her internship soon.

Me: Meet me outside when you're done.

Me: I have plans for us.

Athie: You do?! 👀

Athie: I'll be down in a couple mins!!

The barista placed two hot chocolates on the counter. "Charlie!"

After scooping them up, I kicked open the door and stepped out onto the cold Pittsburgh sidewalk. People rushed to catch the bus home while others loitered around the square, dressed in black and yellow for this weekend's sports games down in the city.

"I'm in a bit of a sticky situation," I said to Hector.

Hector, who had been reading a text off his digital watch,

arched a brow and looked up at me. "*You*, in a sticky situation? No!" he said, feigning surprise.

Hector knew about my secret side hustle—if I could even call it that.

"Ha-ha," I dragged out. "But I'm serious, and I need your advice."

Hector thrust one hand into his suit pants pocket and sipped on his coffee. "Michelle mentioned that you stopped by Radiant twice yesterday, looking for me. Does this *situation* happen to involve your brother?"

"My brother?" I furrowed my brows. "Why do you say that?"

"Because he's become a member of Radiant."

I gritted my teeth and stopped. "He what?"

That asshole had told me that he was in town for a couple of days. If he became a member of Radiant, then that meant he either planned on visiting more often or he intended to move into the city. And his one deciding factor had to have been seeing Athena. He'd hated the city before.

"So, it's not him?" Hector asked.

"No, it's not him." But maybe it was now.

That fucker was going to ruin everything that I had built with Athena over the past few years. He'd come right in, sweep her off her feet, and steal her from me, like he had done with all my friends since I had been just a kid.

"Is it about Athena?" Hector asked, continuing to walk toward Athena's building. "Heather mentioned that she was acting a bit weird the other night. Things must be getting pretty serious if you're bringing her to Radiant."

"I'm not bringing her to Radiant." At least, I didn't have any plans yet. My hands tightened into fists as Derek flashed through my mind. What if *he* had brought Athena to Radiant? "Why? Did you see her there?"

"Michelle said you reserved a room for next week."

"Michelle has a big mouth," I muttered.

He rolled his eyes. "Tell me about it."

I sucked in a breath and averted my gaze to the sidewalk. "That's actually what I want to talk to you about. I need advice. I reserved that room for a—*ahem*—business meeting."

Hector shook his head. "Damn it, Charlie. I warned you about doing porn."

"I enjoy it, and it makes good money."

"Your family is worth a billion dollars. You don't need the money."

"I'm not going to live off them like Derek does." I flared my nostrils and tried hard not to squeeze the cups in my hands. "Fuck being in their socialite circles too. It's not what I want."

Maybe that was what I had wanted in the beginning of college, but since I'd met Athena … a life outside the city with a couple of dogs sounded really nice. I didn't have to worry about what others thought of me, didn't have to show up at every party. I could go on silly little dates with her and enjoy my life.

Only if she wanted that too.

"What's your problem then?" Hector asked.

"I have feelings for Athena," I said, chewing on the inside of my cheek, "which wasn't a problem until … I think she might have certain types of feelings for me back. I only got into porn because I … I never thought that she'd actually like me like that."

"Do you know for sure?"

"No, but we hooked up."

Hector's lips curled into a smirk. "It's about time."

"You can't tell Heather."

"I won't, but I still don't know what your problem is."

"I know that she wants to sleep together, but I don't know if she has the same kind of feelings that I do. And I've already signed a contract with Nadia to film a scene with her next week, which is why I reserved that room."

"What a *sticky* situation. It's not like you can ask Athena how she feels."

"And ruin years of friendship?!" I exclaimed. "I don't want it to get weird between us."

What if she doesn't feel the same way?

"Besides, if she—"

Before I could finish my sentence, the building door opened, and Athena stepped out. The wind blew strands of her red hair, along with the sides of her pink peacoat, back. I straightened out and cleared my throat.

"We'll talk about this later," Hector said, noticing Athena. "I'll see you tomorrow."

"See ya," I hummed, smiling at Athie as she bounced down the steps.

"You didn't have to wait out in the cold for me," she said, waving to Hector. "How's he?"

"Good," I said, handing her a hot chocolate. "Here."

"Thanks!" She beamed and looked out at the busy road. "Where are we going?"

I placed my cup on the ground, snatched her coat, and twirled her back toward me, and tugged it together to button it for her. "You're not going anywhere without buttoning this jacket up. What did I tell you about going out in the cold?"

"Hey," she said, tucking some hair behind her ear and watching me button it all the way up. "I'm wearing a coat! I just" —she smiled harder, and I couldn't tell if she was blushing or if the cold was too harsh for her pale skin—"maybe got excited."

"For our plans?"

She shrugged and tightened her grip on her bag. "To hang out with you."

Fuck.

Warmth spread through my chest, and my dick hardened.

"So, where are we going?" Athena asked, wrapping her arm around mine and hiding her face behind my shoulder to protect herself from the wind.

"A new mini-golf place opened up a couple of blocks down, and—"

"You're not fucking with me, right?"

A chuckle left my mouth. "No."

While still clutching on to my arm, she jumped up and down. Drizzles of hot chocolate rolled down the sides of the cup from her splashing it everywhere. "Yes! I haven't been in so long! I'm so excited!"

My lips curled into a smile, but the heavy feelings of dread washed away any fluttery feelings I had for her. Hector was right. I needed to talk to her to see how she felt, but I was scared —fucking terrified—she didn't feel the same way or that maybe she liked my brother.

Because it had been a couple of days since he'd visited, looking for me, and she still hadn't said a word to me about him. Usually, she was a chatterbox about her day—which I loved— but something didn't sit right with me.

And I refused to give up our friendship for some feelings that I had for her.

CHAPTER
EIGHT

ATHENA

"A BOX of Junior Mints and Airheads, please," Charlie said to the woman behind the counter, flashing her his pretty white smile and pulling out his leather wallet after he checked us into Purple Starlight Mini-Golf—an indoor mini-golf place that just opened in the heart of Pittsburgh.

I glanced over his shoulder, peeping at a picture of us from three years ago at a Pitt football game. It was the first time we had gone out by ourselves and without our friend group. My chest warmed. I really shouldn't be having all these gooey feelings, but I couldn't stop.

Once the lady handed him the candy, he slipped me the Junior Mints. I smiled and ripped them open, popping two of those chewy mints into my mouth. We walked to the first hole in the indoor mini-golf place.

"How was your day?" he asked.

"Good." I beamed. "Same old, same old. Did you work on your virtual reality thingy?"

"My VR *thingy*?" he repeated with a chuckle.

After dropping my pink ball on the turf, I lined up to take my shot. "Your start-up."

Charlie grinned. "I set up a meeting with a couple of investors to get funding."

"You did?" I exclaimed. "That's great!"

While his parents and grandparents could fund any project that he wanted, I knew he didn't want their money. He wanted to do this all on his own, which was a complete one-eighty from when I had first met him.

That wannabe player had turned into a man sometime along the way.

Once he grabbed a handful of Airheads out of the bag, he chomped down on them and tore pieces off. "I have to fly out to California in a couple of weeks to take the meeting. Wanna come with me?"

Sometimes, it was hard to believe that he had grown up in a billion-dollar family with a silver spoon in his mouth, that he'd traveled the world and stayed in the most luxurious hotels, or that he had grown up with the finest of manners. He acted like the biggest, cutest doofus.

"Only if you want me to," I teased.

We played a few more holes, the conversation easy between us, like it had always been. Thankfully, sleeping together hadn't ruined it or made it awkward. We were still the same, even after he'd been inside me. Twice now!

"So, did anyone come see you today?" Charlie asked on hole six.

I raised a brow. "No. Why?"

He shrugged his shoulders and stayed quiet for a couple more moments.

"I heard that Derek came over the other night. Why didn't you tell me?"

Why didn't I tell him that his brother came over?! Because I have literally done nothing but obsess over the fact that he has been inside me not once, but twice now! All my dirty dreams are coming true, and Derek slipped out of my mind.

I walked up to my pink golf ball and lined my golf club up to it. "I didn't think it was a big deal. He said that he was going to text you and that it wasn't really important."

"It *is* a big deal," Charlie said sternly, which was so unlike him.

I glanced over to see him glaring at the fake green grass while clutching his golf club until the veins popped out in his strong hands. He gritted his teeth like he hated Derek more than anyone in the world.

But he barely ever spoke about him, good or bad.

"Why?" I asked while hitting the ball. "Did he do—"

"I don't want him around you alone."

My eyes widened as the ball spun around the back edge of the hole and rolled out of it. I walked over to it and lined up again to hit it into the hole.

Why was he acting so weird about it?

"It's not like he stayed for long," I said. "Only a couple of minutes."

"Did he say anything to you?"

"Not much."

"Did he flirt with you?"

My mouth dried, and I walked up to my ball. Had Derek flirted with me? Maybe a bit. Had I flirted back because I never thought anything would happen between Charlie and me? I really didn't want to tell him that.

"Not really."

He stepped up to his ball, but didn't look up at me. "But he did?"

"Charlie," I whispered, "nothing happened."

After hitting a hole in one, he pressed his lips together and walked toward me like it didn't matter that he had just hit the ball into the hole in a single hit. Something I had never ever been able to do. Not that I cared, but it was more significant than this reaction, wasn't it?

"That's not what he made it seem like."

"You talked to him?"

"Did you flirt with him back?"

I opened and closed my mouth a handful of times, then settled on, "No."

While I might've flirted a bit—I was terrible at it anyway, so Derek had probably just thought I was acting weird—a little white lie to protect our friendship wasn't that bad. It wasn't like Charlie hadn't told a couple of white lies either.

Last Halloween, he had told me that I looked good in that angel costume. Then, the next morning, when I saw those pictures, I wanted to hurl from how terrible I'd looked. But I had spent three hours stressing out over having nothing to wear.

It had protected me at the time, and this would do the same.

I had no interest in Derek either. Absolutely none.

"It's okay if you did, Athie," he said, friendly again. "We're … friends. You can tell me."

Friends …

Shit, that stung.

"Oh, then …" I sucked in a sharp breath. "Um, maybe a little."

The easy look on Charlie's face disappeared, and his jaw twitched. "Oh, okay. Cool."

Cool? Charlie never said *cool*.

"Yeah, but it was just so he'd leave," I whispered. "Nothing more! Really, he's not even my type."

"You have a type?"

"Yeah …" *YOU!!!* "Derek doesn't fit it."

"Who does?"

Internally screaming! What should I say?!

I shuffled my feet on the turf. "Oh, um, I don't really know how to explain it. Just … nice and funny. Derek seems a bit too self-absorbed for me. You know, it seems like he thinks his shit doesn't stink and ..."

And now I am freaking rambling!

Charlie stayed quiet for a couple of moments, then nodded. "Next time he comes to our place, call me immediately."

"But—"

"Athie ..." Charlie whispered, grasping on to my chin and drawing his thumb across my lower lip—something he had never done before, especially in public. "I don't want anything to happen to you, Athie," he whispered. "You're important to me."

My heart pounded so loudly that I could hear it in my ears. *Important to him?* Of course, only in a friendship kind of way, right? That was what it had to be. There wasn't a possibility that he actually wanted a relationship with me.

Or else ... he would've made a move these past few years.

Or else ... he wouldn't have just called me a friend.

"Nothing is going to happen to me," I said. "Trust me, okay?"

"I trust you, but I don't trust him," he said, and then his voice dropped so I could barely hear it, but I gathered, "not to take you away from me."

My eyes widened slightly, and I moved closer to him. "We'll always be best friends."

"Best friends," he repeated, but the words didn't sound like they usually did.

I wondered if the word *friend* stung as badly for him as it did for me.

He brushed some hair out of my face, his fingers gliding against my skin, and moved closer to me. I stared up at him through wide eyes, my heart racing. We had always been this close in public, but not after what had happened. This somehow felt different because we had actually been together, fucking all over our high-rise.

And I might be having feelings that I shouldn't.

My gaze dropped to his lips, and I pressed my thighs together.

One little kiss wouldn't ruin our friendship, right?

I mean, we had already done more than that, but in public? That would kinda make it feel a little too real. Like it meant more than sleeping with each other a couple of times in private. Like he actually wanted this too.

"You're so pretty," he murmured, gazing down at my lips.

Pretty? He thought I was pretty? Like … *that*?

My insides gushed everywhere, and I curled my hands around his collar to pull him closer and stood on my toes to close the distance. I didn't know why I was doing this here, but I couldn't seem to stop myself. As soon as my lips grazed against his, everything seemed to fall into place, except… he stiffened.

"Ew! Mommy, are they going to kiss?" a kid shouted behind us.

I jumped away from Charlie, my heart pounding in my ears and my face suddenly burning hot from embarrassment. Charlie straightened out his back and swiped his thumb across his lower lip.

"We should continue," I said, keeping my head down. "We have a few holes left."

"Yeah," he said, clearing his throat. "We should."

"We're best friends after all," I whispered to myself. "And best friends don't kiss."

Best friends also didn't fuck each other, but that was a problem for another day.

CHAPTER
NINE

CHARLIE

"STUPID KID," I growled through my teeth as I walked into Radiant the next day.

Athena had almost kissed me yesterday at mini-golf, and some immature brat had to ruin it. She had taken me by surprise and stood on her toes to reach me, and I had wanted her to so badly.

Derek sat on one of the leather couches in the main room with two girls on his arm. I pursed my lips because I was still pissed at him and headed straight for the private rooms. I hadn't reserved one tonight, but I hoped they still had some open.

"Hey, Charlie," Michelle said, flicking through some papers. "Need a room?"

"You have any extras tonight?"

"You're in luck." She grinned. "Room nine is free until midnight."

I nodded, but still lingered by her desk. "How long did Derek get a membership for?"

"Derek?"

"Derek Easton, my brother."

"Oh," Michelle hummed. "I didn't know you two were brothers. You're nothing alike."

"Yeah, he's an asshole," I growled. "Do you know how long?"

"I'd need to go back and check," she said. "I wasn't the one who registered him. Why?"

After sighing, I pushed myself off the doorframe that I had been leaning on and turned toward the hallway to find room nine. "It doesn't matter. But if you see him here with a pretty redhead, please tell me."

Michelle stood and hurried over to me. "A pretty redhead? Ooh, who's this?"

"She's …" I paused and looked over at Michelle, who loved gossip. "Nobody."

Once she placed her arm around my shoulders, she pulled me in tight. "Oh, come on. You can tell me. I can keep a secret."

"No, you can't."

"Sure, I can!" She winked. "And you know I'll pester you until I find out."

"She's just my friend."

"Your friend or …" She wiggled her brows. "*Your friend?*"

I cut my gaze to her. "I don't trust my brother not to hurt her. So, please, tell me."

"Oh, you totally like her."

"I do not."

"Do too."

"Michelle. Com—"

"Oh, you like her!" she squealed, jumping up and clutching my arm. "I've never seen you like this before! All the other girls you've brought here, you've been so uninterested in them that I thought you might secretly like guys."

"What?!"

Michelle beamed and continued jumping like a madwoman. "I want to meet her! When are you going to bring her around?"

She pinched my cheeks. "My little Charlie is growing up and having feelings. *Feelings!*"

"Oh my God," I muttered, pushing her off me. "I have to go."

Before she could ask me any more questions, I ran down the hall and headed for the private rooms. I found room nine and kicked the door open with my foot, dumping my backpack near the door and tugging out my laptop and camera.

I hate Derek.

After setting up on the bed to stream, I tore off my shirt and tossed it on the couch across from the bed.

And I can't believe that Athena flirted with him when he came over. She's mine.

I closed my eyes and gripped my cock through my sweats.

All. Fucking. Mine.

And tonight, I would make sure she knew who she belonged to, that she knew what she would miss out on if she chose him over me.

After lying down on the bed, I stroked my cock through my pants, making it harder. She had been on my other streams, which told me that she had a notification set to remind her when I went live. So, if I turned on my camera and jerked one out for her, she would see it. And if I used her panties that I had stolen from the laundry …

My lips curled into a smirk as I pulled her pink thong out of my pocket.

She would fucking lose it. I knew she would.

Once I logged in to my account, I ignored the alarming number of notifications and DMs and clicked right on Go Live, captioning my stream as, *Jerking one out for you,* so Athena would know it was all for her.

Every time I did this, she was the only woman I could think about. Even when I filmed with other women, I closed my eyes and imagined I was thrusting into her from behind. But nothing could compare to being inside my needy girl.

After I grabbed a bottle of lube from the drawer, I drizzled some over the head of my hard cock. The number of viewers continued to rise on the viewer counter on the right of the screen, and the comments began rolling in, but Athie wasn't here yet.

I brushed my thumb across the head of my cock, wetting it. I could drench my cock in this stuff, and it still wouldn't be as wet as when I was inside Athena. Her pussy was gushing, flooding, sloppy with pleasure.

"Fuck," I grunted, tightening my hand around my cock. "You feel so good, baby."

Comments flooded into the chat, and I tried to scan them all to find her name.

A guttural groan escaped my lips. "I know you think of me too."

Will she say something today? Or is she embarrassed that I now knew it was her?

My hand tightened around the base of my cock, and I reached underneath to grip my balls, wishing that it were Athie's cunt they were slapping against and not the back of my hand. The way she had felt in my hands, quivering against me as she came …

"Rub that pretty pussy for me," I murmured. "Oh, baby, I know you can go faster."

I wanted to eat her out so badly, but last time I had ever tried something like that with another girl, she'd pushed me away and told me that I sucked at it, which was why I usually just fucked my partner's throat on live. If I did it with Athena and screwed it all up …

I'd never live that down.

Knowing her, she'd tell me that I was great at it so she wouldn't hurt my feelings.

"I want you a desperate, fuckable little mess, choking on my cock," I growled, "trying to pull away as I thrust it deeper into you, holding on to your hair so you can't go anywhere. Eat your pussy until it's crying all over me."

The pressure grew higher inside me, my abdomen tightening when I thought of making my best friend a dirty little slut just for me.

The thought of her perfect, innocent face, absolutely fucking destroyed every night.

Her grinning up at me with a face full of cum …

Except I hadn't had a chance to cover it yet. All I wanted was to fill up her tight hole.

She was the only woman I'd ever come inside of, and that was the *only* place I would put my cum unless she begged. And even then, it was so hard to pull out of her once I slipped myself in. She felt too good.

I scanned the comments again and nearly froze when I saw Nadia's name pop up on the screen.

Fuck.

ATHENA

"SO, how's it going with Charlie?" Heather asked, eyeing me down.

Heather, Sierra, Sun, Evelyn, and I sat in the middle of Carnegie Coffee Shop—a cute café just outside the city. Usually, they closed at six in the evening, but they had an event tonight and decided to stay open for a couple more hours.

I inhaled the scent of coffee and sipped my iced tea, thinking about Charlie yesterday.

"Good," I said with a smile. "We went to mini-golf last night."

Heather wiggled her brows. "Not *monster* mini-golf."

"Monster mini-golf?" Sun asked, brows furrowed all innocently. "What do you—oh."

"She means his big dick." Sierra giggled.

Sun's cheeks reddened, and I snickered because this was a perfect opportunity to get our conversation off Charlie and me and onto Sun and the person—*people?*—that she was seeing. Besides, I didn't know how to answer any questions about us anymore.

Before, I could say that we were just friends, but we were really more than that now.

"Sun surely knows about monster cocks," I hummed. "Don't you, Sun?"

"And nice titties." Heather giggled.

"Guys!" Sun cried, slinking down in her seat. "Keep it down."

Sierra leaned forward and sipped her hot chocolate, a silver collar glimmering around her neck. "Spill the tea. We want to know what happened when you went to Radiant the other night!"

Sun shot me a playful glare for turning the conversation to her, then bit back a smile. "It was, um, good."

"I heard through the grapevine that you got dicked down."

"What?!" Sun exclaimed. "Who said that?!"

Heather smirked. "Michelle."

"Who's Michelle?"

"Steven and Hector's sister," Sierra said.

Sun placed a hand over her face. "Oh my gosh."

Evelyn—the fifth and most recent addition to our friend group—smiled from the end seat. "Oh, don't make her feel too bad. I remember my first time at Radiant. I didn't know how intense it was going to be, especially with more than one person."

"This wasn't her first time at Radiant," I said.

"Yeah, she's a regular." Heather beamed.

"I am not!" Sun exclaimed, face bright red. "I've only been twice."

Sierra grinned. "Did you get with both Russ and Maya this time?"

Instead of denying it, Sun slinked back again and giggled. "No ..."

"Oh my God, you totally did," Heather teased. "How was it, living my dream?!"

"Your dream is to fuck a married couple?" Sierra asked. "Wait until Hector hears that."

"No!" Heather exclaimed. "I mean, sleeping with another girl."

Sierra wiggled her brows at her best friend, who wiggled them back, as if they were planning to get their boyfriends to agree to something that they probably would never agree to otherwise.

My phone buzzed, and I glanced down at it to see a notification.

7 minutes ago.

AdonisHung is live.

Eyes widening, I quickly turned my phone over so nobody else would see it and sat up taller. Charlie was live now? It was only eight o'clock in the evening! Was he at home? Did he decide to use this time while I was out?

I wanted to watch. He hadn't been live since the night before we slept together.

After shooting up from my seat, I shrugged on my coat and hurried toward the exit of Carnegie Coffee Shop with my phone. "I have to take this! I'll be right back. Please, watch my stuff." My horny ass couldn't wait.

Once I slipped into the car, I locked my car doors and thanked God that it was dark outside because I was about to embarrass myself if it wasn't. I clicked on the notification and logged in to my account.

When he popped up on the screen, I spread my legs as widely as I could in the driver's seat and shoved my hand into my pants, finding my clit through my panties. I closed my eyes for a brief moment and moaned softly.

God, he's so hot.

I reopened my eyes and rubbed my clit even harder and faster, the sensitive bud swelling underneath my touch. On the screen, Charlie had his hand wrapped around his huge cock and was stroking it hard and fast, grunting and cursing to himself.

"Fuck," he hissed, taut abdomen flexing. "Fuck. Fuck. Fuck. Fuck. Fuck!"

When I caught a glimpse of something pink around his cock that he was using to jerk off with, I slowed down and stared at the screen in a haze.

"I want to get you fucking pregnant," he growled, making the comments go wild with horny women—and men. "Come inside your panties and make you wear them all around the city so you know who you belong to."

My eyes widened when I realized that the pink thing wasn't a toy …

Holy fuck, he's using my thong to jerk off!

A wave of heat exploded through my core, driving me higher more quickly than I'd thought. I rubbed circles faster and faster. My phone shook in my free hand, but I continued staring at the screen.

He was using my panties.

He was talking to *me.*

Fuck! The thought of him wanting me so badly that he used my panties to get off!

The pressure built higher and higher inside me, and my knees jerked up around the steering wheel as the pleasure exploded inside me. I threw my head back and screamed out in ecstacy in the middle of the parking lot.

How-how is this happening?! Did he enjoy sex with me that much?

My gaze fell to the comments.

BigTitLoverr54: Can't wait until you do a scene with Nadia.

A scene with Nadia? Who was Nadia? And why was Charlie doing a scene with her?

I stared in a haze at the screen for a few more moments, trying to come up with any answers in my postorgasmic state. But then another comment dropped in the comments section, and I froze.

NadiaLove: Soon.

NadiaLove: I CANNOT wait for you to be inside me. 😢
NadiaLove: I've been waiting for so long!!!

My eyes widened, and the orgasm that I was drifting away in suddenly dropped me back into a harsh reality. I tapped on Nadia's name, which led to her profile on the platform, and tears welled up in my eyes.

When I scrolled through her videos that she had uploaded in the past few weeks, my stomach dropped. She was beautiful—long brown hair that always seemed to be in the perfect blowout, an entrancing siren's gaze, curves in all the right places, and the type of full tits that Charlie always had in his videos if he was filming with someone.

I furrowed my brows, eyes burning, and continued scrolling through her videos.

They were supposed to film a scene together? When was this supposed to happen? This week? Next? Maybe later tonight? He'd said that he wouldn't be home until late tonight. Did that mean he was with her now?

Her page had been viewed millions of times, and she had several hundred thousand people subscribed to her channel.

I swiped away a tear that slid down my cheek. How could I ever compete with her?

It was impossible.

My chest was flatter. My body was slender but straight. Most days, I just threw together a semi-cute outfit and tossed my hair up into a messy bun with some slight makeup to cover my pimples that I was still getting deep into my twenties. And my blow-job skills didn't come close.

What was I thinking?

I sat back against the driver's seat. This was never going to go anywhere. He needed someone to get off with, and I was there with him, horny because I had all these feelings for him. But we really were just friends who had turned into fuck buddies.

We would never be anything more.

CHAPTER
ELEVEN

ATHENA

"THAT'LL BE ten dollars and forty-nine cents. Cash or card?" the barista at Mug Shot Café said.

"Card," I said, yanking open my tote bag and searching inside for my wallet. After last night, I had decided to sleep over at Sun's place because I really couldn't go back home and face Charlie. I had way too many emotions over us. "One sec …"

Damn it! Where is my—

Before I could find my wallet, someone tapped the screen with their card from behind me, the scent of woods drifting through my nostrils.

"Don't worry, babe. I got it."

My eyes widened, and I looked up at Derek, who was now leaning against the counter with a small smirk across his face, ordering a drink from the barista, who giggled at how charming he was.

After straightening myself out, I found my wallet and pulled out twenty dollars. "Here."

Derek stepped away from the counter and walked toward the pickup area with me, slipping his wallet back into his suit pants pocket and shaking his head. "Put that away," he said with a small smile. "It's my treat."

"Come on. I can't owe my roommate's brother any money," I said. "Take it."

By the way Charlie had acted the other night at mini-golf when he asked about his brother, I'd thought for sure that he liked me more than friends or fuck buddies. Even last night, while he was recording, I thought he was talking to me. Hell, he had used *my* panties.

But ... I wasn't sure anymore.

Thankfully, Derek grabbed the twenty from me and folded it, but didn't put it away. Instead, he leaned back against the wall and played with the money, folding it and unfolding it, his smoldering hazel gaze on me.

"You coming to the party?" he asked.

I arched a brow. "What party?"

Derek drew his tongue across his teeth, his gaze darkening. "Charlie didn't tell you?"

My entire body tensed, and I thought back to seeing *her* name on Charlie's stream last night. Whatever party Derek was talking about, Charlie had definitely not invited me, which meant that ... maybe he'd invited her.

"No," I said, pushing my shoulders back, as if it didn't bother me.

We were friends after all. Nothing more.

"Of course he didn't." Derek shook his head and clicked his tongue. "Our parents are having a party later this month. Asked us to bring dates. I thought he was for sure going to bring you, but last time I saw him, he said he wasn't interested in you like that."

Ouch. I bit my tongue. *That hurt.*

"But ..." Derek started with a smile, his cologne becoming stronger as he leaned closer to me. "I'd love to take you out, buy you a nice dress, and bring you to the party as my date." He brushed his fingers against mine.

"Can't have a pretty girl like you sitting at home, all alone."

My cheeks warmed at the compliment, and I looked down at the empty space between us. "Oh, no, no, no. I'll probably be busy that night anyway. Work has really picked up lately, and I'm sure if Charlie doesn't tell me about it, then he doesn't want me there anyway …"

"Who cares what he wants?" Derek hummed. "And you can take a day off, can't you?"

"No, not really."

Derek leaned back against the wall. "How much do you cost a night?"

"What?!" I exclaimed, my face growing hotter. "I don't work as a—"

A low chuckle escaped his mouth. "I'm asking how much your job pays you for a day. I'll give you a week's worth of pay for you to consider it."

Eyes widening, I shook my head. "Oh, no. Really, I'm fine. They don't pay me anyway."

"They don't pay you?"

"No, it's volunteer work."

"For what?"

"Physical therapy."

"Why do you volunteer there?"

Charlie had told me to tell him the next time that I spoke to Derek, but I was having way, way, way too many conflicting feelings inside me right now. I didn't know whether to shut my mouth or agree to go with him just out of spite.

"Hmm?" Derek asked, his fingers brushing against mine again, giving me tingles.

I gnawed on the inside of my cheek. "When I was younger, I was hanging from the monkey bars at school, and I, um … had an accident, a brain aneurysm. I fell and hit my head on a metal slide. And I …" *Fuck, I'm info-dumping again.* "And I was in physical therapy for years, learning to walk again, so this is my way of … paying them back."

While I expected a typical player response from Derek—he seemed like the *uninterested in women's stories and only wanted to fuck kind of guy*—his eyes softened, and his mouth fell ajar slightly.

"Wow," he whispered. "That must've been so hard for you."

After shrugging, I glanced back at the pickup area, where my drink and breakfast still hadn't come out yet. It was only a few bucks, but I felt like I had to stay and talk to Derek as a thank-you for paying for my meal, even after I paid him back.

"Is that why you have a limp?" Derek asked.

My eyes widened, and I snapped my gaze back to him, my cheeks red and flaming and so, so hot. He … he had noticed my limp? I had worked for years to be able to walk, never mind without a limp.

"I'm only asking because Charlie said you had one," he said, holding his hands up as my chest seemed to tighten in on me, squeezing me so hard that I thought I couldn't breathe. "I haven't noticed it though, so I wasn't sure."

Maybe that was one of the reasons that Charlie didn't want to pursue things with me further.

I thought my walk was seamless now. I barely even thought about my accident anymore.

But—I glanced down at my legs—if someone watched me closely, I knew I still didn't walk as straight as I had before the accident. Now, thanks to this little conversation, I would be hyperaware of it for the rest of my life.

"Oh," I whispered. "Um, yeah."

"Who gives a fuck about what he thinks?" Derek said, waving it off like it was nothing.

What does he mean by that? Charlie has confided in him about me, about my accident? He has an opinion on it, on the way I walk maybe? Maybe I was fuck-buddy material, but not girlfriend material. Would he feel embarrassed to be with me like that?

He had never been scared to be seen with me before, but all we had been was friends. When I stood on my toes and tried to kiss him at mini-golf, he didn't kiss me back. Instead, we just went back to golfing after that stupid kid ruined it.

But maybe that stupid kid had saved me from heartbreak.

"Besides, he's too busy with all the other girls in his life."

"What do you mean by *all the other girls*?" I asked, brows drawn together.

"Nadia."

"Nadia?" I repeated.

"Hot coffee. Black!" the barista said from behind the counter.

At the sound of his order being called, Derek kicked himself off the wall and stepped toward me. "Think about the party," he said, lifting the twenty-dollar bill I had given him and stuffing it between my lips. He leaned close to me, so his mouth brushed against my ear. "That's not the only thing I'll shove in your pretty little mouth if you come with me."

TWELVE

CHARLIE

I PACED AROUND our apartment and looked at my phone for the hundredth time this morning. Right now, I was supposed to be in a meeting, but I hadn't seen Athena since yesterday, so I'd canceled it in hopes that she'd be home before her volunteer work.

Me: Have you seen Athena?

I had been texting all of her friends this morning, but I'd barely gotten a response.

Suddenly, my phone buzzed.

Sun: She slept over at my place last night and left about an hour ago.

After rubbing my forehead and wondering why the hell she hadn't messaged me to let me know where she was, I placed my hands on the kitchen island counter and blew out a breath. At least she was safe.

Someone fumbled around with the lock on our front door, and then Athena walked into the room, her long red hair thrown into a messy bun while she wore some of Sun's clothes. She yawned and dumped her bag on the ground, not saying a word to me.

"Where were you?" I asked from behind her.

She jumped up and placed her hand over her heart. "Charlie! You scared me."

I stepped toward her. "Why didn't you come home last night?"

After opening and closing her mouth a handful of times, she shook her head. "I … was …"

"I was worried about you," I said, closing the distance and grabbing her hand. "You always tell me where you are. You left me in the dark all night. I thought something had happened to you, and I—"

Suddenly, Derek's cologne hit me like a fucking brick.

Athena pulled her hand away from me and hurried to the kitchen. "I was at Sun's place."

Sun's place? Sure, Sun told me that lie, too, but Athena could have asked her to.

"All night?" I asked, chest tightening.

She grabbed a glass and filled it with water, her back turned toward me. "Yes."

"You weren't at Derek's?" I asked.

Athena tensed. "No."

"Well, you smell just like him."

Athena spun around, her brows furrowed together in anger like I had never seen them before. "Why do you care what I do, Charlie? It's not like we're together. We're just friends. That's all we've ever been."

Fuck, that stings.

I balled my hands into fists. That fucker could never keep his hands to himself. It was one of the main reasons that I had stayed away from any family function, especially why I shielded Athena from them.

She would have a fucking ball dancing all night at my family's parties, but I would risk Derek stealing her away from me.

He had taken everything from me. And Athena was supposed to be mine and only mine.

After regaining my composure because I couldn't blurt out that I loved her—she had just made it clear that we were only friends—I straightened myself out and cleared my throat. "I only ask because Derek is a bad influence."

Her gaze softened for a moment, then turned down. "That's it? That's the only reason?"

"Yes," I lied. "That's it."

She stared at me for a couple of silent moments. "I don't think he's that bad."

I pulled my gaze away from her, gritted my teeth, and looked out the windows that overlooked the city. *What did he tell her about me? And why would she believe anything that came out of that idiot's mouth? She's smart.*

"He invited me to be his date at your family's party," she said.

"Did you accept?"

"Not yet."

My heart pounded quickly against my rib cage, and I wanted to whisk her away and never bring her back, take her someplace filled with all her favorite things—lizards and tire swings and making those scented soaps she saw all over social media—so she'd see that nobody knew her the way that I did, so she'd want me and not him, so she'd give me a chance.

I had thought that after she found out about what I did, that after we had sex, that after she watched me jerk off with her panties last night and whisper all those dirty things to her, that she would see I wanted her more than anyone in this entire fucking world.

But we were *just friends.*

"Are you going to accept?" I found myself asking.

"No," she said, turning away. "You didn't tell me about it— not that you have to, but it's obvious that you don't want me to be there. So, I'm not going to go with him. Have a good time with your family."

"Athie," I whispered, walking toward her. "I want you to go."

"It's okay," she hummed. "You don't have to lie."

"I'm not lying."

She blew out a long sigh, as if she didn't believe me. "Charlie, I—"

I grabbed her hand from behind. "I'm not lying, Athena."

"Then why didn't you tell me about *it*? You tell me everything."

"I don't like my family," I said. "I wasn't even planning to go."

She gripped on to her glass of water tighter, dropping her voice. "That's not what I mean."

Furrowing my brows, I stared at her and shook my head, confused. She had asked me why I didn't tell her about the party, and I had given her a reason. Was there something else she had expected me to tell her?

"What do you want me to say?" I asked.

She set her glass down on the counter, her breathing heavy. "Nothing. Never mind."

"Are you okay?" I asked, brushing some hair off her shoulder and dipping my head to kiss it. I placed my hands on either side of the counter beside her, trapping her in so she couldn't run away from me. "Did he say something to you?"

"I'm fine."

"You're lying," I said in her ear, resting my head against hers. "Why are you lying to me?"

"What if I did go with him?" she asked, twirling around and crossing her arms. "Hmm?"

"If you're going to the party, you're going with *me*. Not with him."

"You?" She glared up at me through her brows. "Why would I go with you?"

"What did I tell you?" I growled, snaking my hand around the front of her throat and tugging her flush against me.

She sucked in a breath, her pretty eyes growing wide. I pressed myself against her stomach, my nose traveling up the column of her throat.

"You'll go with me because you're mine, Athie. Not his."

CHAPTER
THIRTEEN

ONE MOMENT, Charlie was pressing me into the kitchen counter, and the next, he was dumping me onto his mattress. I landed with an *umpft* and sank into his silky black sheets, staring wide-eyed at him crawling between my legs.

He yanked off my bottoms and placed my thighs on his muscular shoulders.

"Wh-what are you doing?" I whispered, staring at him between my legs.

He placed his mouth on my cunt, and I tugged on his arm.

"I haven't showered yet, Charlie," I said. "I don't know if this is a—"

"You're mine," he growled, sprawling his hand across my stomach to keep me lying down. He fastened his mouth over my clit and flicked it over and over with his tongue, pushing me toward the edge. "Not his."

"Charlie … Charlie, I … Charlie—oh my God!" I exclaimed, pleasure exploding through me. I dug my heels into the mattress and lifted my hips, the tension way more intense than anything

I'd experienced. "Oh my God! Oh my God! You have to stop. It feels too good!"

Instead of stopping, Charlie double downed and shoved two fingers into my pussy, thrusting them in and out about as quickly as he had fucked me the other night. I curled my toes, my legs jerking up to my chest.

"Charlie!" I cried out, gripping his hand, my eyes closed. "Oh my God!"

While I had never had sex before Charlie, I'd had my fair share of guys eat me out, but nobody had even come close to this. I laced my free hand into his hair and tugged, the ecstacy rising higher inside me.

Most guys couldn't even find the clit, but Charlie knew exactly how much pressure to put on it, the tempo, fucking everything. I closed my eyes and tried not to think about how he knew this—because he probably did this with every other girl, but I had never seen it on video.

"Fuck, you taste so good," he mumbled against my clit, finding my G-spot and starting to massage it with his fingers plunged deep inside me. He stared up my body from in between my legs. "Nobody else had better be tasting your pussy."

"No," I said in a breath. "Nobody."

"Good," he growled, pushing me higher. "Because it's mine."

"It's yours!" I squeezed my eyes closed. "Now, please ... don't stop! Don't stop! Don't—"

Fuck!

Pleasure pumping through my core, and my body began trembling uncontrollably. I squirmed in his hold, desperate to displace all this intensity coursing through my body, but Charlie kept his mouth on my clit and his fingers against my G-spot.

"You think I'm done with you?" he growled when I came down from my orgasm, slapping my clit and rubbing the sensitive bud even harder. He sat back on his knees and twirled me around onto my stomach. "Did you think I'd let you off by coming once?"

"Charlie," I said in a daze, the pleasure still pumping through my body. "Charlie, I—"

"You're mine," he said, movements becoming needier, more desperate as he peppered kisses up and down my shoulder and tugged off my clothes. "Mine. Mine. Mine. Mine. Mine. Mine. You're all fucking mine, Athie."

He ruffled around with his pants behind me, tugging them down and pulling out his phone. My pussy tightened, nipples hardening against the pillow at the thought of him—

He opened his streaming app and hovered his finger over Go Live—

Oh God!

"Tell me to stop, and I'll keep you all to myself," he murmured, shoving himself inside me, his mouth against the crook of my neck and his words soft but hungry. "Tell me not to turn on this stream and show everyone that you're mine. That you and this tight little cunt belong to me."

Before I could stop myself, I tapped on the Go Live button myself because I wanted to show that girl Nadia that Charlie was mine and that I was his. I didn't want her to see him again. And I especially didn't want them to film together.

I wanted Charlie all to myself.

Suddenly, I saw myself on the screen, my red hair in my flushed face.

Charlie drew his nose up the column of my throat and stuffed his face into my hair, his mouth against my ear. "Look at you. So desperate to show the world who you belong to."

He wrapped a hand around the front of my throat and pulled me off the bed slightly, pounding into me from behind. My tits bounced, but they definitely weren't as nice as Nadia's or anyone else he had slept with that his viewers probably—

"You know what you're going to do for me to make up for that lie earlier?" Charlie murmured into my ear. "Stop taking those pills. Toss them in the trash."

"What pills?" I asked, the pressure building higher in anticipation.

"Your birth control."

"My birth control?" I repeated, my heart racing, and suddenly, the awareness of the camera was gone. While hundreds of people were now watching, all I could think about was that Charlie had just said *birth control*! "You want me to …"

"Yes," he said, leaning forward slightly so I came back down to rest on my belly. He grabbed a fistful of my hair and tugged back on it so I looked directly into the camera. "Tell them what you're going to do," he growled into my ear.

I stared into the camera, my pussy tightening around his huge cock, which was pounding deeper and deeper inside my pussy and driving me mad with pleasure. "I'm going to throw away my birth control so you can get me pregnant."

"That's right." He gestured toward the camera. "That's right; you're going to watch me fill this slut's pussy up with cum today. The first and only girl I've come inside of." He gently nibbled on my neck. "I'm so hard, thinking about how much I'm about to pump into you."

I clenched harder around him, my pussy pulsing uncontrollably.

"I meant everything that I fucking said on live last night," he said. "Make you take every last drop of my cum, make you mine, breed you, get you pregnant. Even when we have a family, I'm going to breed you every fucking night so you give me more kids."

Holy shit. Holy shit. Holy shit!

"You're going to take my cum in your pussy every night." He pounded into me from behind, his mouth all over my throat and his fingers squeezing my nipples. "My goal is to get you pregnant before that stupid fucking party."

"Please give me it," I cried. "Please!"

He put the camera right in my face, showing off my blotchy cheeks, and shoved a couple of fingers into my mouth, which I sucked on like a willing little whore. "Look at you, you filthy little slut, begging for my cum."

"Please, come inside me," I pleaded, slobbering on his fingers. "I need it."

"You need it?" Charlie asked from behind me, his husky voice in my ear.

"Yes," I whimpered, the pressure at the very edge. "I need it!"

Charlie propped the phone up against the headboard, then wrapped his arms underneath my thighs and lifted me into the air, giving the camera a perfect view of his cock buried in my pussy. I sat helplessly in his arms, desperate and aching.

"Look at the way that pussy just swallows my dick," he growled. "So hungry for it."

His fingers found my swollen clit, and all he had to do was brush them against the bud to send me moaning and screaming and trembling in his arms. An orgasm ripped through my body as my pussy milked the cum out of his balls.

Cum suddenly started rolling down his cock and balls, spilling out of my cunt and ruining his sheets. "Your pussy is drooling, baby." He trailed his nose up the column of my neck. "With my cum."

I cried and bit down on my lower lip so I wouldn't say his name. He finally pulled out of me, letting his huge dick swing down and smack against his thigh. With me still in his arms, he showed everyone his cum drooling out of my pussy, a low chuckle escaping his mouth as he looked at the screen of comments.

BigDickRon: Fuck!

Suxmydix2: Best creampie I've seen!

UnknownBigTitsLover3: Fuck her throat next time.

Freddie69: Plug her up.

BigDickRon: Make that dirty slut walk around with your cum all day!

Bunnie34xx: Don't let it go to waste. 😰

"You see that?" Charlie purred into my ear. "They want me to plug up your pussy." His cum dripped off my pussy lips, but Charlie caught it on his finger and stuffed it back up inside me, pushing it as deep as he could get it. Then he grabbed my panties from the bed and pulled them up my thighs. "Let's pull these panties up. So you have to sit in them all day, thinking about me. So you remember who you belong to."

CHAPTER
FOURTEEN

CHARLIE

ONCE I SHUT off the camera, I lay back on the mattress, next to Athie, and stared up at the ceiling, breathing heavily. All sorts of gooey feelings that I hadn't felt for anyone before seemed to gush through my chest, and I just wanted to tell her that I loved her.

Not as a friend, like I usually did.

But that I truly fucking loved her. That I really wanted to get her pregnant and that it wasn't some fantasy to breed my best friend and that I really had thought about having a family with her one day.

Suddenly, a sob echoed through the room. I snapped my gaze over to Athena, who was curled up into a ball all the way at the edge of the bed, with her hand over her mouth and tears streaming down her cheeks.

Immediately, I sat up and moved next to her, taking her into my arms.

"Did I do something?" I asked, her face in my hands and my eyes searching her trembling ones. I furrowed my brows, confused because, a second ago, she had been into everything that I was saying. Maybe I'd pushed her too far. "Did I say something? What's wrong, Athena? Talk to me, please. Why are you crying?"

What was going on? I'd thought that was how she wanted me to treat her in the bedroom. I thought that she wanted me to be a little rough, claim her mouth and pussy. Her body seemed to want it. At least, that was how she had made it seem …

Instead of answering me, Athena cried harder, her shoulders bucking forward.

Maybe it was the way that I had eaten her out. Had she not liked it?

God, why am I so bad at it?

"Did I hurt you?" I whispered, searching her body for any marks that I might've left. I jumped out of bed and headed for the door. "I'm going to get you some water, start the kettle for some tea. I …"

I stared at her for a couple of seconds, then hurried out into the hall to get her some water because I had no idea what was going on. Nothing like this had ever happened before to me during or after sex. And to see those tears fall from *her* eyes … possibly because of me …

Fuck, what have I done?

After starting the kettle on the stovetop, I filled a glass of water and hurried back to the bedroom, my heart racing. Athena had sat up, her legs hanging off the side of her bed, the blankets wrapped around her shoulders, hunched over.

I should've taken more time with her before flipping on my phone and starting that stream. Maybe she felt like I'd pressured her into doing it. Maybe she hadn't wanted to be on camera. I could've ruined her law career before she even started it.

Once I reached her, I held out the water for her, but she didn't take it. So, I set it on the nightstand and crouched in front of her. Wet tear trails decorated her face, but no more tears were leaving her eyes.

"What's wrong?" I whispered.

She stared at me and shook her head, as if to tell me she didn't want to talk.

But I wasn't having it.

"Did Derek say something to you?" I asked, trying to stay calm, but Athena had been acting weird ever since she had gotten home, and I smelled his cologne all over her. He had to have something to do with this.

She shook her head again, but the tears began once more.

Athena pulled the blankets up to her chin and stared at me through watery eyes, not saying a word. I waited and waited and waited, so she knew I wasn't going anywhere until I knew she was okay.

"Don't you have to work?" she whispered.

"No."

"Yes, you do."

I set my hands on her knees and shook my head. "No, I'm not leaving you."

"But—"

"Tell me what he said."

"He didn't say anything. This … this isn't about him."

After blowing out a low and controlled breath—because she was lying to me again—I sat beside her on the bed and cupped her chin in my hands, desperate for her to tell me what was going on. "Talk to me, Athie. What's wrong?"

She opened and closed her mouth, lips quivering. "Do you think I walk weirdly?"

"No," I said, furrowing my brows. "What would you walk weird from?"

"My accident."

"Your accident?" I repeated.

Sure, sometimes, she didn't walk straight, and she had a bad habit of walking into me while we walked down the road, not balancing correctly when she stood for a long time, but I had never once thought it was weird.

And I would never mention it to anyone anyway. Why was she bringing this up?

"Why would you think that?" I asked.

She looked away and shrugged. "I don't know. I just look weird."

"No, you don't."

"I'm so clumsy," she said, shaking her head. "I don't know who will respect a lawyer who limps around everywhere and—"

"Stop it, Athena," I said. The words came out more sternly than I'd expected, but I was sick of her putting herself down.

When we had first become friends, that was all she did. And she had worked hard to feel confident in herself. And now, for some reason, she was like this again, and I wasn't having it.

Athena stared up at me, her eyes widening even more. "But—"

"That experience might've shaped your life, but you're more than that," I said, wondering why the hell this was coming up now. "Why do you care about what anyone thinks of you anyway?"

She looked down at her lap, voice dropping. "Because ..."

I waited for her to continue, but she didn't after a few moments.

"Because?"

"I don't care about what *just anyone* thinks of me," she said.

But she obviously did care. At least, she cared about what I thought if she was asking me this. But never in my life had I ever *intentionally* done anything to make her think otherwise. I loved her for who she was, not what she looked like or how she walked.

"You don't understand," she whispered, tugging the blankets around her body. "I l—" Before she could finish her sentence, she smacked her lips closed and looked down at her knees, bouncing them up and down, her cheeks reddening by the moment. "Never mind."

"What is it?" I asked, lowering my voice and grabbing her hands. "You can talk to me."

"Not about this," she whispered, glancing over to my computer. "I … I can't."

"If you can't talk to me, then at least tell me why you think this all of a sudden. Was it your little run-in with Derek? Did he say something to you about me? Is that why you don't want to tell me about it?"

"No!" she exclaimed, but she couldn't look me in the eyes. "I was just thinking about it …"

I balled my hands into fists, ready to kick his ass for good this time because Athena was lying to me. I could hear it in her voice, could see it in her expression that she tried to hide from me. Derek had said something to her, and I planned on teaching him a lesson.

Nobody messed around with my girl.

CHAPTER
FIFTEEN

ATHENA

I BLEW out a breath and stared emptily at the law textbook in front of me. While I needed to prepare for the bar that I had next month, I couldn't think about anything other than what had happened earlier in Charlie's room.

Between wanting to breed me to talking about my limp, had he been telling me the truth?

"Okay," Heather said, slamming my book closed. "What's up?"

"Nothing," I said, shrugging it off and not even peering in her direction.

When I tried to open the book, Sierra peeled it away from me and stuffed it into her black bag. I glanced up to see Heather, Sierra, Sun, and even Evelyn staring at me and waiting as if I had something to spill.

"Did something happen with Charlie?" Evelyn asked.

My cheeks warmed, and I looked away. "No."

"Oh my gawd!" Heather exclaimed. "Spill the deets."

I sank further in my seat. "Nothing happened, Heather."

I had just completely embarrassed myself in front of Charlie, crying and sobbing because I was insecure. He had helped me get over my insecurities when we first became friends, and I felt so silly, still being insecure about them now.

But I couldn't help it, all right? I had the biggest crush on him, and I wanted him to like me too.

Heather leaned forward, eyebrows raised and intense gaze on me.

"Okay, fine!" I exclaimed, wanting them to drop it. "We kissed."

Instead of throwing a grand celebration like I'd expected, they all stared at me for the longest time, with the blankest faces, as if they didn't believe me. I furrowed my brows and picked up my tea, sipping it.

"You're lying," Heather said.

"Why would I lie about—"

Suddenly, Heather grabbed Sierra's shoulders and shook her violently. "Did you hear that? Or am I hearing things?! Because I know that Athena didn't just say that she and Charlie kissed with tongue!"

My cheeks warmed. "Heather! I did not! And can you stop being so loud?!"

Sun scooched closer to me and lifted her brows. "But did you though?"

Somehow, my body felt even warmer, and I pressed my legs together underneath the table to suppress the ache between them. I shuffled my feet against the floor and chewed on the inside of my cheek. "Maybe …"

Heather placed her hand to her heart and faked fainting against Sierra. "It keeps getting better."

Evelyn leaned toward her. "Next, she'll say they fucked."

I sank down in my seat. Heather would have a field day with—

"Oh my God," Heather whispered, staring at me. "I'm going to have a heart attack."

I hid my face behind my hands for a moment. "You're so dramatic."

Heather rolled her eyes. "I'm literally hyping my girl up, and she's calling me dramatic?!"

"I'm just … embarrassed," I whispered, wrapping my arms around myself.

"Why?"

"Because I overreacted with him this morning."

Evelyn rubbed my shoulder. "It was your first time, so there's no reason to be embarrassed."

"It wasn't my first time. We've been sleeping together for—"

Heather clapped her hands together, her happy expression dropping. "If this bitch says they've been sleeping together for months and she didn't tell us, my head will actually fall off my shoulders."

"It's only been a couple of days," I said.

"A couple of days?! Why didn't you tell me last night?" Sun exclaimed.

"Because I don't know if it's even going to go anywhere, and I don't want it to get awkward in our friend group." I pressed my lips together and dropped my gaze to my piping hot tea. "I don't know if he wants to be more than friends or not. He's giving me weird vibes."

"How so?"

I shrugged. "I tried to kiss him in public, and I don't know, I got the feeling that he didn't want to."

Sierra furrowed her brows. "Is that all?"

I thought back to the entire Nadia situation, but thought better of myself than to share that Charlie was a porn star and that I was his most recent guest fuckdoll. I really, really, really didn't want them to go searching it up and seeing me naked!

"Sorta …" I whispered.

Sun drew her finger around her cup lid. "It's so obvious that he wants to be with you."

"Sure, maybe physically," I whispered. "But I don't know about emotionally."

Maybe he had been hesitant about being a couple because of how emotional I was, especially after I broke down in tears right after the best sex of my life. He'd probably thought he had done something wrong or overstepped a boundary.

And I just couldn't get out of my freaking head!

"And you said that *I'm* being dramatic," Heather said, playfully rolling her eyes.

"My thinking is perfectly logical," I hummed, though I knew it was clouded with insecurities from my limp to Nadia—especially Nadia.

"All right, girls," Carol, the barista, said from behind the counter. "We're closing up soon."

I gathered my belongings and shoved them into my backpack, my lips tugged into a frown. Maybe I just needed to get out of my head a bit. Charlie and I had been best friends for few years now.

If he didn't want to be seen with me, then he wouldn't go out with me every chance that he got. If he didn't like me, then he wouldn't pick up my favorite cheesecake and take me on mini-golf dates and help me make strawberry soaps on Saturday nights.

"I have just the thing to get your mind right," Heather said with a mischievous grin.

I arched my brow. "And that is …"

"We're going out."

"In the middle of the week?" I asked, slipping my bag over my shoulder.

"Hell yes!" Heather exclaimed, jumping out of her seat and grabbing my hand. "And I know just the place. If you don't think you're hot, then we'll make sure you know you are. Tons of guys will be crawling all over you tonight."

"What?!" I exclaimed. "I don't want that!"

"Oh, come on." Sierra gently elbowed me. "If Charlie isn't

going to admit his feelings to you, then you have to make him. Get him jealous so he claims you while everyone is watching."

The girls began giggling like it was their fantasy.

But they didn't know that what she had just described … had happened today.

"Where are we going?" I asked, trying desperately to go home. "Isn't it too—"

Evelyn snatched my cup of tea from the table as the girls dragged me to the door. "We're going to Radiant."

CHAPTER
SIXTEEN

CHARLIE

THE BITING cold seared my cheeks. I pulled my coat together and walked down Pittsburgh's icy sidewalks toward Radiant, seething. I had been looking all around the city this afternoon and evening for that stupid fucker, called his phone countless times, and even asked the few friends that I knew he had in the city just to find him.

After tugging open the door and walking past security, I shook off the snow from my coat and slipped out of it, and then I handed it to the attendant. She gave a small smile with a curt nod, depositing the coat in the back room.

I scanned the lobby for Derek because he had to be here somewhere.

Where the fuck else would he be? I had made sure to keep a better watch on the security cameras at my place, in case he decided to pay me—or Athena—another visit tonight while I was out looking for his ass.

When there was no sign of him, I walked down the hallway and toward the main bar area. Maya and Russ—Sun's … *friends* —were together at a table in the back of the bar. Michelle was sitting on a table with a submissive, trying to butter her up. Steven and Hector stood near the bar with Abdul, talking quietly and chuckling with each other.

Abdul nodded to me. "Your usual?"

"No, thanks," I said, grinding my teeth. "I'm not drinking tonight."

"Someone looks pissed," Steven noted, sipping his drink.

I balled my fists and scanned this room for that asshole. "Have you seen my brother?"

"Brother?" Steven asked, looking at Hector.

"That asshole kid from yesterday," Hector said.

Steven let out a long whistle. "He's your brother?"

"Yes," I said through my teeth. "Have you seen him?"

"He was here last night," he said. "Got a little too drunk and handsy. Arrogant bastard."

"Ooh," Michelle hummed, squeezing herself between her adopted brothers to see me. "Are we talking about Charlie's cute little crush that he has?" She clapped her hands together, giving us a huge grin. "I wanna meet her!"

"No, we're not talking about my crush," I said through gritted teeth.

"So, she *is* your crush!"

I peeled my gaze away from Michelle and peered at Hector, who glared at her, and Steven, who gave a little chuckle.

"Don't you have a business to run?" Hector asked. "An event tonight?"

After whipping out a dildo from behind her back—*don't ask me where she got it*—she grinned widely at him and shoved it into his chest. "The event was a success, and we had some extra dildos left over if you ever want to"—she wiggled her brows—"you know, use it on yourself."

Flaring his nostrils, Hector grabbed the dildo between two fingers, walked over to the trash, and dumped it right into it without an apology.

Michelle melted to her knees. "My precious merchandise!"

"If you didn't want it to go in the trash, you shouldn't have given it to me."

"You could've used it with Heather, not thrown it away!"

"I have enough toys for Heather."

Michelle stood and smirked. "You can never have too many toys. Right, Steven?"

"Have you seen Derek?" I asked, butting into their conversation.

If I didn't get Michelle to stop talking soon, I would be stuck there forever while she talked all about sex, sex toys, and why we all needed them to keep things spicy in the bedroom. As if Steven, Hector, and I didn't already use them.

Mid-sentence, Michelle paused and looked over at me. "Your brother?"

"Yes."

"He was here last night," Michelle said, looking at the brothers. "You didn't tell him?" When the others didn't say anything, Michelle threw her arm around my shoulders and pulled me in close. "Didn't know sadism ran in your family."

"Sadism?" I repeated through gritted teeth. "What'd he do?"

"Had some girl crying so loudly that we had to go check on them."

My heart raced, and I balled my hands into fists. "It wasn't Athena, was it?"

Was that why she had started crying after sex earlier? No, it couldn't be. I would've noticed marks all over her body. But still … if he had been here with someone last night and I smelled his scent all over her …

With every second that passed, I became more and more enraged that Derek would say something to Athena about me or about her, making her insecure in her own body, trying to put a wedge between us. Or worse … actually hurt her.

"No, it wasn't Athena," Hector said. "Some woman with pink hair."

"But it was red by the time they left," Steven hummed.

"Not judging them," Michelle chimed in. "But we all thought something was wrong."

I ran my hand over my face and blew out a breath, calming down—only slightly—now that I knew it wasn't Athena. Derek hadn't hurt her yet, but if he had been practicing at Radiant … I feared that, one day, he might try to convince her to do something that she didn't want to do.

Coerce her by using her insecurities against her.

"If you see him or Athena, please text me."

Michelle smiled and pinched my cheek. "Look at you, little lovebird."

After shoving her hand away, I pursed my lips. "I'm not in love with her."

Lie.

Steven and Hector shared another chuckle, as if they didn't believe a word I'd said while Michelle rocked back on her heels and scrunched up her nose and eyes.

"You remind me of Steven when he met Sierra for the first time. Lying to yourself."

Hector sipped on his drink. "He's not lying to himself. He's lying to *you*. Big difference."

"Damn, what is it? Bully Charlie Day?" I asked.

Michelle giggled. "Yes."

When my phone buzzed in my pocket, I whipped it out in case it was Athie.

Nadia: Who was that girl in your stream earlier???

Nadia: And why have you been ignoring my messages?

After staring at the texts for only a moment—because I couldn't handle any shit with her right now—I turned off the screen and slipped the phone into my pocket. Nadia could wait until I found Derek and kicked the shit out of him.

"I think I'm going to—" I started.

"So, you're just going to ignore my texts?!" someone exclaimed from behind me.

I turned my head to see a woman dressed in a slutty pink dress, storming toward us.

Nadia.

ATHENA

"I DON'T LIKE IT HERE," I whispered to Evelyn after I stripped off my coat and handed it to the nice lady at the coatroom.

I awkwardly shifted from foot to foot and scanned the lobby, which looked *relatively* decent.

At least there wasn't any sex going on yet.

"You'll get used to it," Evelyn said, handing over her coat.

"Get used to it?!" My eyes bugged out of my head. "I will not!"

Sun snickered to herself. "You see what Heather got *me* into?"

I playfully glared at her. "I will not be involving myself in a sex club on a normal basis."

Heather walked over to us with a huge grin. "That's what they all say."

"It's not going to happen," I said, crossing my arms. "Trust me."

After hooking her arm around Sierra's, Heather walked to the left, where music drifted out of the room. I dragged my feet but continued after them because I did *not* want to be left here alone. What if someone tried to hit on me?!

"This is the main club area," Heather said, stopping at the door.

I peeked my head in quickly, saw two older women sitting on this young guy's lap with his arms around their waists as they felt up his hard cock, and then stepped back. No way did I want to see more.

This is so embarrassing!

Watching porn and seeing it in real life were two waaaaay different things, and I hadn't prepared myself. I had twenty entire minutes to psych myself up in the car, but I hadn't thought I'd be this awkward about it!

Hell, Sun came here alone.

"I can't believe you come here—like, at all!" I said to Sun, my arm locked around her elbow.

Sun was the sweetest and quietest out of all of us, and somehow, she'd met a couple at a sex club?!

"There are naked people!"

Sun giggled into my shoulder. "You should see the glass rooms."

My eyes widened. "What happens in the glass rooms?"

Heather popped her head between ours and threw her arms over our shoulders, steering us from the bar area and down a separate hallway, where men, women, and couples, scantily dressed, lounged on couches, drinking and kissing.

I gulped, unable to believe that I was here.

"Sierra's classroom was down that hallway," Heather noted, nodding to a hallway that we passed. "That's where she lost her virginity to her professor."

Sierra playfully slapped Heather. "Not everyone has to know!"

"Doesn't feel too good, does it?" I giggled, loving that it wasn't *me* on the spot now.

Evelyn nudged Sun. "Did you see Maya and Russ? They're in the main room."

Sun's cheeks reddened. "They are?"

"Yep," Evelyn said. "Bet Maya's jealous that you're with us."

Sun tucked some hair behind her ear. "They don't like me like that."

"Mmhmm," Sierra said.

At the end of the short hallway, Heather stopped and turned around. "You ready?"

"No," I said.

What were these glass rooms anyway? Definitely nothing good.

"Too bad," Heather said, yanking me toward her.

She dragged me down the next hallway, where there were several huge glass rooms—some that we could see into, some that we couldn't, some that were vacant, and some that had a handful of people fucking every single hole in that room.

"Oh my God," I whispered, pussy beginning to ache.

"Isn't it so hot?" Heather asked. "Imagine fucking Charlie in one of these."

My cheeks reddened even more. "Can they see us?"

"It depends," Heather said. "If they want to see you, they can. If they don't, they won't."

"How does it work?"

"There's a remote inside the room. You can make the glass completely transparent—transparent from the outside, transparent only from the inside, or not transparent at all."

"Depends on what the couple is into," Sierra said. "Some people like to be watched. Some like the thrill of seeing other people while getting it on. Others don't want to see or be seen at all."

I sucked in a breath, my nipples hardening. If Charlie ever brought me here, I would want people to watch, but I wouldn't necessarily want to see them. The thought of other people getting off because of me … made me excited, but the thought of seeing them in real life … not so much.

Online, sure. They could get good angles with a camera.

Some guy inside one of the rooms nodded at the group of us, beckoning for us to come in. My eyes widened, and I dug my heels into the ground in case Heather decided to try to get me to go into one of them.

That was *not* happening—ever.

Well, maybe not *ever*. Maybe with Charlie.

My entire body warmed at the thought of being in one of these rooms with him—the walls on the inside dark so that I couldn't see out, but transparent on the outside so that everyone could see in and watch us have a good time.

It'd be just like … earlier.

Nipples hardening underneath my shirt, I crossed my arms to hide them and chewed on the inside of my cheek.

Would Charlie even ever consider coming to a sex club like this? Probably, but how would I even bring that up in our conversation?!

Hey, I think you might like me. Wanna go to a sex club?

Bruh, I would die from embarrassment if that came out of my mouth!

"I'm going to get a drink," I said, speed-walking back to the exit of this place.

I needed to take a break or else I would combust from horniness over how much I wanted that man. It was unhealthy, but on the way over, Sierra and Heather had really convinced me that Charlie just didn't want to overstep.

That had to be it, right?

He didn't want to ruin our friendship, just like *I* didn't want to ruin our friendship.

Once I made it out of the hallway of glass rooms and through all the kissing couples, I stepped into the main bar area, where we had kinda, sorta started. I blew out a low breath, thankful that there weren't *that* many naked people fucking in all kinds of ways here.

No shame to them, but this was the first time I'd seen this many naked people in real life.

I found an empty seat on one side of the bar and slid up onto it.

"What would you like to drink, hon?" the bartender said.

I eyed his name tag, which read *Abdul*, and smiled. "Anything."

"Anything?" he repeated with a smile, a single lock of his dark, curly hair on his forehead. "You sure?"

"Yes," I said, relaxing against the back of the seat. "Anything's good with me."

All I needed was to get drunk or at least tipsy so I could get through tonight or to give me the courage of slipping out of here while I had the chance so my friends wouldn't introduce me to blood play next.

"That's a dangerous thing to say to me," Abdul said, placing down a napkin and adding alcohol to a drink to make it a pretty pink color. He placed it in front of me and grinned. "What do you think?"

I sipped on it slowly, the sweetness calming me. "It's really good."

"House special." He beamed. "Let me know when you need another."

"That'll probably be soon," I said.

My gaze drifted around the bar aimlessly until I spotted Steven and Hector standing awkwardly on the other side of the bar. I furrowed my brows, wondering what was going on, but then my gaze moved to the couple behind them.

Charlie.

Eyes widening, I stopped mid-sip and stared at him. No, I had to be seeing things. Charlie wouldn't come to a sex club. At least, not without me, right? The girls had hyped me up so much tonight that I … I thought that Charlie actually wanted me and only me.

I shifted my focus from him to the girl beside him, tears welling in my eyes.

A pretty girl, a foot shorter than him, chocolate hair, brown eyes, and more cleavage than I even had boobs.

Nadia.

ATHENA

MY HAND SHOOK as I set the drink down as calmly as I could. I blinked a few times, because surely—*surely*—this wasn't what I thought it was. This … I … I had to be seeing things. Was that really Charlie with Nadia?

Almost as if he knew I was watching him, Charlie looked over at me.

And it truly sank in that what I was seeing was real.

His face contorted from shock to confusion. When Nadia wrapped her arm around his and pressed her tits against his biceps, I shoved back my chair and shuffled back on my feet, unable to take my eyes off him.

I … this … he was really here.

Tears welled up in my eyes until they burned. Pain shot through my chest. I turned around and ran away as fast as I could.

"Athena!" Charlie shouted behind me. "Wait up! It's not what it looks like."

But I didn't care what it looked like. I cared about what I had seen with my very two eyes.

Charlie is out at a sex club with Nadia.

I pushed through the crowd of people, ran through the lobby, and slipped out into the cold before anyone could try to stop me. My legs moved faster than my mind could really, truly process what was going on.

What was I even thinking?! Of course he would be here with her. They were going to record a porno together. Charlie wouldn't have brought her back to the apartment. He would've hidden her from me.

My eyes burned, and my chest tightened.

Why had I believed that Charlie would be different from every other guy? All he wanted from me was some pussy. I was just an easy friend he could sleep with, one he had taken advantage of, knowing that I enjoyed watching his videos.

Rain poured down around me as I ran down the sidewalk, blindly making turns at corners and not keeping track of where the hell I was going. All I knew was that I needed to get as far away from there as possible.

The January cold seared my cheeks. I wrapped my arms around myself because I had forgotten my coat back at Radiant and continued to weave around people when they exited restaurants and bars in the city.

"Woah, whoa, whoa," someone said, catching my waist and pulling me underneath a door awning to keep me out of the rain. "Where are you running off to? It's pouring outside, and you don't even have a coat on."

I sniffled and wiped my cheeks, lifting my gaze to see Derek.

"Oh, um …" I said, my voice hoarse. "Nowhere."

He took my face in his hands and lifted it. "Are you crying?"

"No!"

"What's wrong?" Derek asked, searching my face and not letting me go.

I opened and closed my mouth a handful of times, not being able to utter a single word until, finally, the only word that I was able to get out of my mouth was a measly, a broken … "Charlie."

"Did he do something to you?" Derek asked.

"No, I'm just …" I stared at him, trying to hold back the tears because I didn't know him like that and Charlie and I … we weren't even a thing. "I just …" I opened my mouth, expecting to finish my sentence, but a sob escaped it.

I slapped a hand over my mouth to muffle the noise. I needed to get out of here.

But before I could twirl around and run back out onto the rainy sidewalk, Derek wrapped his arms around my shoulders. I tensed in his arms—because this wasn't right; Charlie had told me to stay away from him—but his hug felt so good.

My arms wrapped around his torso, and I pulled him tight to me, crying into his shoulder. I probably looked so stupid—I sure as hell felt it—but Charlie … I had thought we were … I had been so naive, so stupid!

Charlie was at a sex club, about to film a scene with Nadia.

And right after we had sex this morning …

"Thanks," I said once I finally pulled away. "But I should get home."

Could I even go back home?! Did I want to face Charlie right now? Honestly, not really.

Maybe Sun would let me sleep over at her place again. Heather and Sierra both lived with Hector and Steven, so they didn't even have an apartment together anymore. Which really only left Sun's place and my place.

But I had left Sun at Radiant. She was probably with Maya and Russ or the girls.

"How are you getting home?" Derek asked.

I pursed my lips. "I'll walk. It's just a few"—*dozen*—"blocks."

"No, it's not." Derek pulled keys out of his pocket. "I'll drive you."

After eyeing the keys and wondering if this really was a good idea—Charlie had warned me to stay away from him, but I was such a mess right now that I didn't even know how to get back to Radiant from here, and I'd left my coat there—I nodded.

"Okay," I whispered. "Just home."

His lips curled into a soft smile—the warm kind Charlie usually had with me. "Where else would I take you?"

Once I shrugged, he grabbed my hand and led me to the car right on the street, opening the door for me to slip into the passenger seat. I sat down and smoothed out my bottoms, which were soaked through from the rain.

Derek sat in the driver's seat and started the car. "Where were you?"

"At a bar," I whispered.

"Downtown?" he hummed. "Which one? I've only been to Radiant and a couple others."

"You've been to Radiant?" I asked to keep my mind off Charlie.

"A few times," he murmured, glancing over at me when we stopped at a red light. "You?"

"That's, um"—I gulped and looked out my window—"where I just came from."

"*You* were at Radiant?" he asked with a chuckle.

I looked over at him. "What's so funny about that?"

"You're too innocent for a sex club," he said. "When I left you this morning, your cheeks were about as red as your ass would be if you had gone to Radiant with me tonight."

Suddenly, warmth spread through my body. I pressed my thighs together, and Derek definitely noticed. The thought of being hurt in any way didn't get me all hot and bothered, but another guy thinking I was attractive in that way did.

Especially if Derek preferred to flirt with me rather than Nadia.

"Why were you at Radiant?"

To make Charlie jealous, and I ended up getting my heart broken.

"My friends brought me," I said.

"And you ran out, crying about Charlie?"

Shit, I forgot I'd cried his name.

"Um ..." I started, shuffling my legs together. "Yeah."

"You tried to make him jealous and saw him there with someone else?"

I snapped my gaze over to him. "How'd you—"

"If you want to make him jealous, be with someone he doesn't like."

"He likes everyone ..." *Except you.* "What are you suggesting?"

Derek drew his thumb across the leather steering wheel. "You know what I mean."

My heart pounded so loudly that I could hear it in my ears, but the thought of dating Derek to make Charlie jealous seemed to fly out the window as soon as Derek drove underground into the parking lot underneath my apartment building.

He parked in a visitor spot and shut off his car, but I didn't even attempt to leave the car. My legs bounced against my hands, and I swallowed hard. What would I say to Charlie? He knew I had seen him there.

Honestly, I didn't care that he had been at the club—all of our friends went there—but he was there with her. Maybe he even took her back to our apartment. What would I do if she was in the middle of my living room, riding Charlie on our couch?

Had she been at our place before? Maybe. And if she had, there was no doubt that he fucked her on every inch of the place. She was so pretty that no man would ever resist her, not even Charlie.

"I'm sorry for making you drive all this way," I whispered. "But I can't go up there. Not now."

"Where do you want me to take you?"

"Anywhere," I said, tears burning my eyes again. "I don't care. Anywhere but here."

CHARLIE

"ATHENA!" I shouted, shoving past people in the club to follow her out.

Fuck, this looked bad. Really bad.

If Athena knew who Nadia was, it would make this all even worse.

Athena's red hair disappeared past the doors, and I continued to push people out of the way, only to be stopped by someone's hand wrapping around my wrist and tugging me back. I hit the edge of a couch and twirled around.

Pissed and upset.

But what the fuck was Athena doing here anyway? At a sex club? Alone?! Had she come here to find me? To make me jealous? I didn't know, and I wasn't sure that I wanted to find out. What if she had been here with someone else?

Derek perhaps.

"Are you really running after that ugly bitch?" Nadia asked.

Her words made me freeze in my tracks, my entire body shaking in anger. I balled my hands into fists so tight that my nails cut into my palms, my vision blurring. "What the fuck did you just say?"

Nadia crossed her arms. "Why are you running after that ugly bitch?"

I would never lay my hand on a woman out of anger, but when those words came out of Nadia's mouth … boy, I had to stop myself from doing just that. I blew a breath out of my nose and stepped closer to her.

"If you say anything like that again about Athena, I'll fucking destroy your career," I snarled, taking another step closer and glaring down at her with so much more hatred than I'd ever had. "I will destroy *everything* you have. I don't care how dirty my hands get from it. I don't care how much money it'll take. I'll make sure you're nothing to the world."

The smug expression on Nadia's face suddenly disappeared, and she shuffled back.

"Don't you dare insult her ever again—you understand?" I snarled.

All she could do was nod, and I refused to spend any more time making sure that she did. She had one fucking warning, and if she crossed the line again, I would make good on my promise to her.

"Charlie, where are you going?" Nadia asked. "What about our scene together?"

"Take a fucking hint," I shouted through gritted teeth. "It's not happening."

Nadia grabbed my elbow and yanked me back. "We have a contract."

I ripped myself away from her. "Fuck the fucking contract."

Once I slipped out of the main room toward the lobby, I bumped into Heather and Sierra with Sun and Evelyn in tow. I scanned the area, seeing no sign of Athena, which meant she had probably run out of here.

And I didn't blame her.

If I had seen her with another man at a sex club, I would lose it too.

"Charlie," Sierra said. "What are you doing—"

"Leaving." I pursed my lips and twisted my head to look back at Nadia, who pouted near the bar, her dress way too tight for her body, screaming desperation. "See that girl in the pink dress? She told me that Athena was ugly."

"She what?" Heather exclaimed, gritting her teeth.

While I couldn't hit a woman, I knew Heather had no problem with it. She wasn't one to get into fights, but her boyfriend owned this club, and I knew she wouldn't take anyone's shit who hurt her friends.

"Oh, hell no," Heather exclaimed, storming over to her.

The last thing I saw before hurrying out was Heather grabbing a fistful of Nadia's hair and winding her fist backward. I snatched my coat and keys from the coatroom and hurried toward the exit.

When I stepped out of Radiant, wind seared my face. I looked down both sides of the street, hoping that Athena was within walking distance, hoping that she hadn't gotten far. It was dark, and while Pittsburgh was relatively safe … Athena was a pretty girl, and I wouldn't doubt that someone would try to pick her up.

"Athena!" I called over the harsh wind. "Athena!"

Nothing.

I slipped into my car and double-checked the security cameras in our apartment to make sure that Athena hadn't gone home yet. Once I was sure, I started the engine and drove down the streets, one by one, slowing down by any young woman to see if it was her.

It was dark, cold, and raining, and I doubted that Athena would stay out here long.

While driving, I called her phone over and over and over, but it went to voicemail every time. Everyone who was close to her was at Radiant, which meant that there was only one person left to call.

The dickhead that I had been calling all day, who refused to answer.

Except this time, he did on the first ring.

"Didn't think you loved your big brother this much," Derek hummed, amused on the other end. "Calling and texting me all day. The desperation really, really doesn't suit you. Maybe that's why Athena stayed over at my place last night."

That bastard. That fucking bastard!

"If you know where she is, tell me," I growled. "I don't have time for your games."

"Games?" Derek repeated. "If I was playing games with you, you'd know it."

I flared my nostrils and glared out at the street, seeing smears of lights blazing down the road. "Cut the fucking shit and tell me where she is." I balled my hand into a tight fist at the mere thought of Athena with him.

Of him using her at her weakest.

"Saw her earlier, running down the street and crying," he said, and I could just hear the smile on that fucker's face. "That could've been the rain, so I asked her what happened, and she asked me to bring her back to my place."

"If you've—"

"Of course, as your big brother, I couldn't betray you like that," he said like he was some god. "I know you've got the biggest crush on her. So, out of the kindness of my heart, I brought her back to your apartment."

"You're lying," I said through gritted teeth.

"I did bring her back to your apartment." He paused with a slight chuckle, like my life was some sort of wild comedy to him. He had probably set this up from the start. "Not my fault she didn't want to get out to see you."

"I'm not going to ask you a-*fucking*-gain. Where the fuck is she?"

In the background, I heard some shuffling, then a female's voice. "Derek?"

"Go back to sleep, baby," Derek cooed. "I'll be there in a minute."

"If you fucking touch her, I will kill you," I shouted, slamming my fist against the steering wheel because I could do nothing. This was all my fucking fault. "I'll fucking kill you!"

CHARLIE

WITH THE RIGHT MOTIVATION, I found my brother's address in twenty minutes. I slammed the side of my fist against the door and hollered at him to let me inside. If he had Athena in here, I swore to fuck, I would—

"Damn, no need to be loud," a pink-haired woman mumbled, opening the door.

Before she could slam the door in my face, I stepped into his apartment and scanned the room for any sign of Athena. She fucking had to be here. She had been here when I called. Where was that fucker hiding her?

"Where is she?" I snarled.

"Where is who?" Derek asked, walking out of a room with a towel hanging around his shoulders, another fastened around his hips, and beads of water rolling down his chest.

I shoved him out of the way and hurried into the room.

"Athena," I called.

The bathroom was empty.

I gritted my teeth and briefly looked into the other rooms in this hallway, spinning around when she still hadn't come out after I yelled her name. Was she that pissed at me? Did she really not want to see me? She would surely let me explain, right?

"Where the fuck is she?" I growled, shoving my brother into the wall. "Huh?"

"Who?"

"Athena!"

"Oh, her."

Before I could stop myself, I slammed my fist into the side of his face. He stumbled back against the wall and swiped the corner of his lip with his thumb, wiping away the blood. He stared back at me through hooded eyes, his pearly-white teeth covered in blood.

"You like her that much?" Derek hummed. "I can tell you that she doesn't feel the same."

"Shut up," I snarled. "Where is she?"

"She cried in my arms when I picked her up off the street like the dirty whore she is."

I hit him again, this time so hard that he fell to the ground. And when he opened that stupid fucking mouth again, I dropped to my knees, grabbed two handfuls of his hair, and slammed his head on the floor.

And all that fucker did was laugh.

"Next time I see her, I'm going to fuck her until she screams for me to stop."

Slam.

"I bet her pussy is tight as fuck if you're this obsessed with her."

Slam.

"You wish she loved you like you do her."

After another slam, the pink-haired bitch got between us and pushed me back. I held back my fist because I wasn't going to hit her and get thrown in jail—I really wouldn't find Athena then— and stood.

"Relax," she said. "Who are you looking for?"

"The girl he just had over," I growled.

She helped Derek to his feet, but he pushed her away. After rolling her eyes, she shook her head and walked to the couch, grabbing a pack of cigarettes.

"Sweet girl," the pink-haired girl said, opening up the door to the balcony and lighting up a cigarette. She puffed on it and blew it out the door, drawing her silky purple robe together. "Don't know where she ran off to though."

"So, she was here?" I asked, cutting my gaze to my brother.

Derek raised his hands, as if he had done nothing wrong, and I stared at him for a few more moments to figure him out. He liked Athena, and if he had her alone, of course he would try to do something with her.

He wouldn't have brought her all the way here and not made a move.

Once I finally broke my glare, I stormed to every single room in his apartment, yanking open all the closet doors, looking underneath all the beds, pulling out all his shit to see where he had hidden her.

She had to be fucking here.

"What the fuck are you doing?" Derek shouted, following me around, but not attempting to stop me. He might've been my older brother, but he knew I would kick his ass if I found her here. "I already told you that she's not here."

"Where did she go?!"

"She left." Derek shook his head. "Why don't you fucking believe me?"

I twirled around, grabbed him by his neck, and slammed him up against the wall. "I don't believe you because you've been trying to fuck up my life since we were kids. And there isn't a better time to do that than now, when I've finally fallen in love with a girl."

The words slipped out of my mouth before I could stop them. It was the first time I had said it aloud—I had thought it a million times—but to hear those words ... it was jarring. I had never loved anyone the way I loved her.

And when I'd finally gotten close enough, she was gone.

Derek's lips curled into a smirk. "You love her?"

Flaring my nostrils, I shoved him back and stormed out of the room and to the front door. The pink-haired girl flicked her cigarette out onto the balcony and closed the doors, her robe now drenched in rainwater.

"If I see her, I'll holler."

"Please, fucking don't," I murmured underneath my breath.

I didn't need Athena running around with someone like Derek or her, who apparently liked torture. It would've been completely fine, but I really, really didn't like her fucking vibe. It gave off *predator*.

And I didn't want her convincing Athie to try being a masochist for Derek.

So, I left. And when I had absolutely nowhere else to turn, nowhere else to check, and nobody else to call, I drove back to the apartment and parked in the underground lot. I pressed my lips together and tried to hack my brain for something— *anything*.

Where could she have gone off to? Why hadn't she answered any of my calls? Was she that angry at me? Would she let me explain? And would she believe me if she did give me the chance? She had been so sad at Radiant when I locked eyes with her.

My clothes stuck to my body from the rain. I stepped onto the elevator and hit the button to close the doors. I paced inside it and ran a hand through my hair, my mind buzzing.

"What am I going to fucking do?"

The elevator stopped on the main floor, and the doors opened.

Halfway into the elevator, the woman stopped. I lifted my gaze to see the woman I had been looking for all night, her cheeks stained with tears and her eyes wide as she looked at me.

"Charlie ..."

My eyes widened twice as much as hers did. "Athena ..."

CHAPTER
TWENTY-ONE

ATHENA

I OPENED and closed my mouth a handful of times, standing in front of Charlie with tears in my eyes. The elevator doors shut behind me, and I gulped down all my words.

What do I say to him? Right here? Now?!

"Athena," Charlie whispered again.

After shuffling next to him, I turned toward the elevator entrance. The lights above the door lit up with every passing floor, and I desperately needed it to hit ours now. I didn't know what to say to him.

At Derek's place, I'd had him call me an Uber almost immediately. He told me he would pay for it, too, since I'd left my belongings at Radiant and that I could pay him back later. So, I had been driving around Pittsburgh for the past hour while an old guy listened to me cry.

Never once did I think about what I would say to Charlie!

"Athie," Charlie said, taking my hand. "I'm—"

My first instinct was to pull away. So, I folded my hands together and shifted from foot to foot, my heart pounding so loudly that I could barely hear the sound of his voice. I knew it wasn't the right thing to do …

But I didn't want to blindly fall for his charm.

As soon as he started talking, as soon as he touched me, I would melt.

And that couldn't happen tonight. I needed answers so badly. I needed to know that he and Nadia … that they were … a couple, so I could forget all about him and about the way he made me feel—because what had I been thinking?

Honestly? He was waaaaaaay out of my league, and I couldn't date a porn star. No matter how good of friends we were. We should just be friends and nothing more. That would solve all my problems.

I glanced up at the door.

Floor seven. Floor eight.

We were whizzing up to our floor, yet time seemed to move so slow.

Floor nine. Floor ten.

Just two more.

Floor eleven. Floor—

Before the *12* could light up above the door, the elevator suddenly stopped. I glanced at the door, waiting for it to open, but instead, the elevator remained stagnant. I pressed on the button for the twelfth floor several times, but with no success.

Charlie tapped on the Door Open button, and nothing.

"It's stuck," I muttered to myself. "Why is it stuck?"

God, this is just my luck!

All I had wanted to do was sink into my bed and cry myself to sleep, not get stuck in an elevator with the man I loved, who *obviously* didn't love me back if he had been at a sex club with the girl he was supposed to sleep with!

Tears welled up in my eyes again.

"Don't cry," Charlie cooed, hitting the Call button. "We'll get out of here."

He didn't know I wasn't crying because of this. Or maybe he did. I wasn't going to ask.

My gaze landed on his hand as he pressed the button again. His knuckles were covered with dried blood.

What happened?

He had just been at Radiant with Nadia. Why were his knuckles bloody? Had he gotten into a fight with someone?

"Hello. How can I help?" the operator said through the speakers.

Charlie glanced back at me, but I looked away. "We're stuck."

"We're aware of the issue, and we're working on fixing it as soon as possible."

And with that, she didn't say another word. Charlie stepped back and took a breath. I crossed my arms and glanced over at him, and he looked away right after our eyes locked. He scratched the back of his head and shuffled his feet.

"Did Derek touch you?" Charlie said, breaking the silence.

"Derek? No."

"Are you sure?"

I glanced down at his bloody knuckles. "Did you hit him?"

"Are you sure he didn't touch you?" Charlie asked again, ignoring my question.

Which meant that he'd totally hit Derek. It must've been right after I left because I hadn't been gone from Derek's house for more than an hour, an hour and fifteen minutes tops. Had he tracked me down after spotting me at Radiant?

"He didn't touch me," I said, and then he went silent. "So, did you record your scene?"

He snapped his gaze to mine. "What?"

"Don't play stupid with me, Charlie," I said, tears trembling in my eyes. I balled my hands by my sides and finally turned toward him. I really didn't want to hear that he had, and I didn't want him to lie to me, but we had to talk about it at some point. "Nadia."

His blue eyes widened. "You know who she is?"

"Of course I know who she is!" Tears fell down my cheeks. "She only shows up in the comments of every single one of your videos, saying how she can't wait for you to finally be inside her." A sob escaped my lips, but I pressed them together. "So? How was it?"

"I didn't do a scene with her," he said.

While I wanted to believe him, I didn't … I *couldn't*.

"You're lying," I whispered. "You're lying to me."

Charlie moved closer and gently grasped my elbow. "Athie, I—"

I shook my head and tightened my crossed arms. "You slept with her."

"No, I didn't."

"You were at a sex club with her, Charlie!" I exclaimed, staring up into his sea-colored eyes. My feelings were all over the place right now. My chest hurt. My eyes burned. "How can I not think that you slept with her when I see the guy I love at a sex club with a girl who's prettier than me?!"

"She's not prettier than you, Athena. Nobody is prettier than you!" Charlie, who had been staring down at me with so much conviction that I might actually believe him, suddenly paused, his eyes softening. "Wait … what did you just say?"

I opened my mouth to say it again, but then realized that I had … I had stupidly told him that I loved him. And all this jealousy definitely screamed that I loved him more than a friend. But he … I …

"What do you mean?" I whispered.

His features softened. "You said that you … that you love me?"

After I gulped down all my fear—because this was the worst thing that could possibly happen—the elevator doors slid open. When they did, I turned on my heel to run out as quickly as possible. I needed to get out of here, to get some air.

It was all stuffy with feelings in here.

But before I could step outside the elevator completely, Charlie seized my wrist, tugged me back inside, and pressed his lips against mine.

CHAPTER
TWENTY-TWO

ATHENA

"I LOVE YOU MORE," Charlie said in an open-mouthed kiss, his lips hungrily all over mine. He pressed me up against the elevator wall and interlocked his long fingers with my smaller ones. "So much more."

Warmth exploded through my body.

Charlie loves me? Surely, I had to be hearing things.

"No, you don't," I whispered to him.

"I've loved you for seven years, Athie," he murmured against my lips. "Seven years."

While I didn't want to believe it—because why hadn't he told me?—I could do nothing but kiss him back. I laced some fingers into his blond hair and tugged on it, my heart racing. This was … really happening!

"Now say it again," he murmured against my lips. "Tell me you love me."

The words sounded almost desperate, as if he had been waiting for me to confess my love for years now, just like I had been waiting for him. I curled my fingers around his shirt, scared if I said it again, then there would be no going back.

"I love you," I whispered, pulling him closer. "I love you, Charlie Easton."

Just before the elevator doors shut, Charlie picked me up with his hands around my thighs and walked with me into the hallway and to our door, his lips never leaving mine once. He hastily tapped his code into the lock and kicked our door open.

After setting me on the counter, he ran his hands up and down my thighs. My pussy was pulsing already, and he hadn't even touched me there yet. He groped my thighs, my ass, and then my thighs again, his touch driving me wild.

"I need you so badly," I whispered.

He trailed kisses from my mouth to my jaw and then down the column of my neck. His stubble tickled my skin. I arched my back, leaning into him and giving him better access, and moaned softly.

"I'm obsessed with everything about you," he murmured against me.

Another moan left my mouth. He wasn't even touching me intimately yet, but I was already so close from just his words. Sure, Charlie and I'd had sex before, but I had never felt like this with him. I had never gotten so close to coming so quickly.

Finally, he moved his hands between my legs. When his fingers met my clit from outside my bottoms, I curled my fingers into his shirt and cried out. Pleasure shot through me, and I raked my nails down his back.

"Every time you come," he said, "tell me you love me."

More heat exploded in my core. "I love you, Charlie. God, I love you!"

"That's my girl." He peppered kisses back up to my lips. "I love you too."

In the midst of an orgasm, I clenched my entire body because his words kept pushing me higher. He drew his fingers faster around my clit and kissed down the center of my chest, pulling my shirt to the side so my small breasts fell out of it.

He sucked one of my nipples into his mouth, flicking his tongue across it.

My eyes rolled back, and I curled my toes. "I love you. I love you. I love you!"

"You're so pretty when you come," he said, gently biting down on my nipple. "I can watch you like this all day."

He continued kissing down my stomach to the top of my bottoms. After pulling them off me, he kissed my inner thigh. My legs began shaking, and I clutched onto his shoulder.

"I need you inside me," I whimpered. "Please, I want to make you feel good too."

Instead of standing between my legs, he pressed his mouth against my clit and shoved two fingers inside me. My toes curled, and I laced a hand into his white-blonde hair, tugging on it with all the tension inside me.

"Please, Charlie … if you don't stop, then I'm going to—"

"This pussy is mine," he said. It wasn't in a possessive, jealous way, like it had always been before. But in a softer way, like he knew it to be true and he wanted to boast and brag about it. "All mine."

The pressure built higher inside me. "Charlie …"

He gently sucked on my clit and looked up at me. "I love you."

Pleasure shattered inside my body, and my hips lifted off the counter. "I love you."

After kissing back up my body, he placed his mouth against mine and kissed me on the lips this time, his tongue slipping into my mouth. He undid his pants as I tried to catch my breath, and then he lined himself up with my entrance.

When he began pushing himself inside me, I pulled away to look up at him, to really admire him. He pushed into me, his eyes much less hazy with lust, like they had been so many times when we were together.

They were more careful.

He glanced from eye to eye, then leaned his forehead on mine. "Do you really love me?"

"I love you." I gently clasped his chin to draw him closer and kissed him. "Do you really love me?"

He wrapped his arms around my waist, picked me up from the counter without pulling out, and walked with me to his bedroom. "More than you'll ever know, Athena."

He set me on the bed and crawled up after me, his forearms on either side of my head on the pillow.

When he began thrusting into me, I grasped the sides of his face and melted into his kiss. Every thrust pushed me higher, and I wrapped my legs around his waist to pull him closer.

Higher and higher and higher, until it was becoming harder to hold myself back.

Before I could release all over him, he grunted into my mouth, "I love you." And then he suddenly stilled.

Pleasure rushed through me, and I cried out in ecstasy again.

CHAPTER
TWENTY-THREE

CHARLIE

THE NEXT MORNING. I fluttered my eyes open. Athena laid her head on my shoulder, her body curled into mine. I breathed in her strawberry shampoo and listened to her soft and slow breathing against my chest.

Gently, I rubbed my fingers against her hip. She stirred against the crook of my arm, then opened her eyes. The sun flooded into the room and hit her blue irises, making them a sea of color.

"Good morning," she murmured, squinting.

"Morning."

She looked down at my lips. "Was last night real?"

I chuckled. "Yes."

"Do you take any of it back?" she asked. "It's okay if you—"

Before she could finish that sentence, I pressed my lips to hers. "No."

A soft smile stretched across her lips, one that made me all giddy on the inside. She giggled and tucked some hair behind her ear. Then she pressed her lips to mine again. "I don't take it back either."

After shuffling back so I leaned against the headboard, I massaged her shoulder in circles. "Why did you suddenly get so insecure about the way you walked?" I asked, unsure if I should bring this up now.

Chances were that if she had brought it up then, she was still thinking about it, still thinking that I would choose someone else over her because some asshole had said something to her about the way she moved.

Athie pulled the blankets up to her chin and shrugged. "I don't know."

"Derek said something to you, didn't he?" I asked, trying to stay calm.

She tensed and gulped. "Yes, but I'm sure he didn't mean—"

"I love how you see the good in people," I said. "But some people aren't good."

Her bottom lip quivered, but I grasped her face before she had a chance to cry.

"I'm sorry," she whispered.

"There's no reason to apologize. Just don't listen to a word that comes out of his mouth."

"I know, but … I had been feeling really insecure over Nadia and all the other girls that you'd been with," she said, dropping her gaze. "I look nothing like them, and he caught me at a bad time."

I didn't want to tell her this—because I honestly didn't want to get into the whole porn thing—but there was a reason that I didn't do it with any girls who looked like Athena. Athena was special to me, and I wasn't going to try to replace her with another woman.

"You don't have to worry about Nadia or any of the other girls. Because there are none."

"But you still have to—"

"No, I don't have to do anything," I said. "No more porn, unless *you're* the girl with me."

She swallowed, her eyes growing wide. "Do you mean it?"

"Yes."

"Really?"

Another chuckle left my mouth. "Yes, Athie. Now, I'll make us breakfast," I murmured against her lips. "Don't move."

It was half selfless, half selfish to keep her in my bed. I wanted her to feel special after she'd confessed that she loved me last night, but I also so desperately wanted to get rid of those pills in the kitchen cabinet. Now.

Instead of heading right for the pantry closet to grab the pancake mix, I glanced behind my shoulder to make sure Athena hadn't followed me and headed straight for the cabinet where she kept her birth control pills.

Once I found them hidden in the back, I grabbed them and walked to the trash. I glanced down at them to see that today's pill was still in the packet. But so was yesterday's and the pill from the day before.

Every single one of them since we had started this little relationship.

My dick hardened inside my pajama pants. *Fuck!*

Athena had always—*always*—taken her pill. Almost religiously. She had multiple alarms set every morning to make sure she took it, but it wasn't like she was having sex anyway.

Now she actually was, and she wasn't taking them.

Fuck. Fuck! Athena wants this as much as I do.

I pushed each of the pills out of the packet, the silver lining breaking and the pills falling right into the trash, never to be found. I did it so every single one of them wasn't in the packet any longer, and then I dumped the remainder of yesterday's coffee grinds from the coffee maker over the top of them.

She had known my goal from the beginning. I had made a promise to her.

And after Derek had decided to take advantage of her, I wasn't taking any chances. Athena was mine, and I wasn't going to let her go. She was stuck with me forever. I'd make sure of it.

I shut the trash can and grabbed the pancake mix from the

pantry, dumping some into our mixing bowl and pretending like nothing had happened. It wasn't like she needed them anyway.

Just the thought of seeing Athena's belly round with my baby …

Damn, it does something sinister to me. Makes me want to tie her up and breed her until she's pregnant.

After adding some vanilla, milk, and eggs, I stirred the contents of the bowl, trying to calm myself down so I wouldn't barge back into my bedroom and take Athie again. I didn't want her to think that I was using her after she admitted all her feelings to me last night.

"It smells yummy in here," Athie said, walking out in my oversize shirt.

Fuck, she knows exactly what she's doing to me. Maybe she always has.

I set the spoon down in the bowl and cocked my finger. "Come here."

Once she reached me, I seized her waist, set her on the counter, and stepped between her legs. She giggled, her red hair falling into her face, and tugged me closer to her, pressing her lips against mine.

I drew my hands up her thighs and gripped her ass underneath my oversize shirt. When she curled her legs around the backs of my knees and pulled me closer, I sucked her bottom lip between my teeth.

"God, you're so sexy."

My dick hardened even more, and I pulled it out, setting it right against her entrance. Athena sucked in a breath, her nipples becoming taut against my shirt. I pulled her closer and pushed myself into her tight cunt.

I would keep my promise to her. She'd be pregnant before my parents' party.

TWENTY-FOUR

ATHENA

"WHERE DID YOU GO LAST NIGHT?" Heather exclaimed, stalking into the apartment with Hector in tow.

She grabbed my hand and dragged me to the other girls, who sat in the living room, while Hector joined Charlie in the kitchen.

Steven was standing over a smoking stove, waving his hand so the smoke wouldn't set off the fire alarm. Hector rolled his eyes at him and pushed him out of the way so the chef could take over making a simple cake.

Some of the guys had decided to join us for our movie day. But I was glad, so I could get some alone time with the girls because I had so much to tell them about last night, especially that Charlie had said ... *he loved me!*

Heather flopped down on the couch between Sierra and Sun. "So?"

Evelyn rocked back on her heels and glanced up from her phone, eyebrow raised.

I grabbed Evelyn's hand and squeezed. "You will not believe it!"

Suddenly, the couch girls sat up taller, as if they were waiting for the tea.

After peeking briefly in the other room to make sure that Charlie was occupied, I grinned and lowered my voice. "Charlie said that he loves me."

"FINALLY!" Heather shouted, jumping up. "About damn time."

Sierra followed. "Did he really?!"

I glanced at Sun, who stood and grinned.

"Yes. And I said it back."

"The sky is falling," Heather said. "You admitted your seven years' worth of feelings!"

"It hasn't been that long," I said, cheeks warming. But really, it had been.

"So, how did it happen?" Sierra asked.

"We were in a fight," I said.

Heather rolled her eyes and giggled. "Classic. Did it accidentally spill out?"

My cheeks warmed even more. "Maybe ..."

"Who said it first?" Evelyn asked.

"Me."

Heather slapped me hard on the arm, as if she couldn't contain herself. "Bitch!"

I burst into a fit of giggles because I couldn't contain myself either. I had been holding it inside all morning, just waiting for all of them to get here so I could tell them everything that had happened.

Heather grasped my elbow. "I'm so happy."

I glanced down at her fingers on my arm, then did a double take because they were bruised. "What happened to your knuckles?" I asked Heather. "They're bruised."

Heather snickered. "You should see the other girl."

My eyes grew even wider. "What do you mean, *the other girl*? You got into a fight?"

The girls all grew quiet—very unlike them—and shared a look.

"What happened?" I asked again.

"Charlie didn't tell you?" Sun asked.

I glanced over at Charlie, who was talking to Hector and Steven. "No?"

"Well, then don't worry about it," Heather said, waving it off. "It's taken care of."

"No, I want to know," I said. "What happened? Was this because of me?"

After they shared another look, which meant that this was *definitely* because of me, Sierra leaned in closer to the group. "Apparently, this bimbo at Radiant said something rude about you, and Charlie basically told Heather to take care of her."

"Bimbo?"

"She wasn't a bimbo," Evelyn said to Sierra, stifling a laugh. "Don't slut-shame when Steven walks you around Radiant like you're his pet."

"I'm not shaming her. It's the best way to describe her." Sierra put up a finger. "The definition of a bimbo is an attractive but stupid woman, and she was definitely stupid if she thought she could say anything about Athena without consequences."

"Consequences meaning my fists," Heather clarified.

They must've been talking about Nadia. I looked over at Charlie, who was always so playful, so innocent—at least that was what I thought—but had he actually told Heather to take care of Nadia for me?

While I didn't condone violence, it made me feel butterflies all over. And I had wanted Nadia to get what was coming to her for a long time. She'd made me feel so shitty about myself, especially when I saw her at Radiant last night.

"What did she say about me?" I asked.

"It doesn't matter," Sun said. "Because it's not true."

"Please, tell me."

"But it's mean," Sun whispered.

"What did she say?"

"She just said that you were ugly," Heather said. "But it's not true."

Evelyn caught my hand. "Apparently, Steven and Hector overheard Charlie and her conversation right after she said it. Charlie said, and I quote, 'If you say anything like that again about Athena, I'll fucking destroy your career. I will destroy *everything* you have. I don't care how dirty my hands get from it. I don't care how much money it'll take. I'll make sure you're nothing to the world."

"How do you remember every word?" Sun giggled.

Evelyn fanned herself. "How do you not?!"

"Oh my gosh," I whispered, pressing my legs together. "That's so hot."

Heather squealed. "I know! So sexy, standing up for his girl!"

A giggle left my lips. While I hadn't heard those words directly from Nadia, I knew she would say something like that about me. I didn't know her, but she seemed like a mean girl who wanted my man.

And now that I knew he loved me, I wasn't going to let anyone have him.

I turned toward Heather. "You didn't have to hit her."

"Yes, I did."

"She totally did," Sierra said.

"Yeah, no question," Evelyn said.

"It was deserved," Sun chimed in.

My lips curled into a smile, and I pulled them in closer because I didn't know what I would do without them. If it wasn't for them dragging me to Radiant, then maybe I wouldn't have told Charlie that I loved him, and maybe he wouldn't have said it to me either.

CHAPTER
TWENTY-FIVE

CHARLIE

TUESDAY MORNING, I shoved clothes into my suitcase. Athena and I were going to fly to California tonight for a meeting that I had with investors, and I had held off on packing until now because I was nervous about it.

This was my first chance to finally separate myself from my family and their money. After what had happened this past weekend with Derek, I had more fire in me than ever to make this start-up succeed. I didn't want to depend on my family and their name forever.

Athena deserved more than that.

I folded suit pants and tucked them away into one of my suitcase pockets. While this was the biggest meeting of my career, I was nervous that I would make a total fool of myself in front of Athie and the investors.

From my limited experience with investors and venture capital, most of them were grimy, disgusting, and only after one thing—taking as much of a company as possible for as little investment as possible.

My lip curled up in disgust from the thought of having to negotiate with retired frat guys like Derek and my father. I flicked through my shirts in my closet and picked three that would match the suit.

While I hated that this was the case, being a man and asking for investment was easier than being a woman and asking for one. The majority of investments went to male-led businesses while less than five percent went to female-led businesses.

Fucking stupid.

I had heard one too many horror stories from my business classes in undergrad about female students who had been bullied by investors who wouldn't stop asking them about their worth after they'd built a million-dollar business.

Someone knocked on my bedroom door, and I looked up from my messy thoughts to see Athena, dressed in a lime-green sweater and some bell-bottom jeans. Her hair was thrown up into a bun.

"Yes?" I hummed.

She chewed on the inside of her cheek. "I have a question for you."

"What is it?" I asked, zipping up one side of the suitcase.

"Have you happened to see my birth control?" she whispered, teetering from foot to foot.

"Your birth control? It's not in the cabinet?"

She sucked in her inner cheek, her bright eyes on mine. "No."

I drew my tongue across my teeth, pleasure and guilt rushing through me. My gaze raked down her body, landing on her hips. Then I grabbed another pair of dress pants from my closet and walked to my suitcase sprawled out on the bed.

"Why are you looking for it?" I asked, looking up. "It's not like you were using it anyway."

Athena's cheeks flushed a bright red, and she averted her gaze and tucked some hair behind her ear. "Y-yes, I was. I just, um ..." She crossed her arms over her chest and shuffled her feet, peeking back up at me. "I forgot to take it the past couple of days."

Once the pants were packed away, I stalked closer to her, took her chin in my hand, and lifted it. "A few days, huh?" I drew my nose down hers, my lips grazing her soft ones. "Since we started this little thing between us?"

She stayed so silent that I could hear her swallow. "Charlie, I … please, don't be mad."

"I'm not mad, Athie," I murmured, swiping my thumb across her lower lip. "After I filled you with my cum the other night, I popped all those pills into the trash so you couldn't take your pills even if you wanted to. And to my surprise, you haven't been."

Athena moved closer to press her lips against mine, but I didn't let her get close enough. Instead, I kept my lips millimeters from hers, the corners of my mouth curled into a smirk. She whimpered against me.

"I'm going to do whatever I have to do," I murmured, "to trap you."

A giggle escaped her lips. "To trap me?"

I wrapped my arms around her waist and pulled her flush against me, lifting her into the air. "Trap you with me forever, Athie." I spun her around and landed on my bed next to the suitcase, her body on top of mine.

She grinned, her nose scrunching all cute, the way it always did when she was happy.

"What's wrong?" she asked, pushing some hair off my forehead. "You're worried."

"I'm not worried."

"Yes, you are. You have that line between your brows, like you do when you're worried."

After letting out a low sigh, I looked away because I was embarrassed. I had never felt embarrassed in front of Athie before, but I didn't want her to think that I didn't have us and that I wasn't going to take care of her.

I had just gotten a taste of her, and I didn't want her to leave me.

"What's going on?" she whispered.

"I'm nervous about this trip."

"About the investors?" She curled her fingers against my shoulders. "You'll do great."

"They're going to be assholes," I said. "I don't want to deal with it."

Athena shrugged. "So what? You don't *need* them. Your business is doing well on its own, and I think you know the market better than anyone, especially with your experience in the … you know, porn world."

Investors wanted a product that would make them hundreds of millions, a product or platform that could be worth billions of dollars. What my team had created could easily hit that mark. But it included elements of porn that made that a bit harder.

Everyone consumed porn in some way, but not many people liked to admit it.

It was an easy market to break into, especially with advances in AI and technology, but there was going to be a lot of credit card charge-backs from husbands and wives who'd been caught consuming pornography by their spouses.

"Stop it," Athena said, using her forefinger and thumb to stretch out the wrinkles that had to be forming on my forehead. "There is no reason for you to stress about this. You're okay whether they invest or not."

"I want to make a good living for us," I whispered, staring up into her light eyes. I gripped her waist and pulled her closer to me. "I want to give you the world without my family's monetary support."

"I don't need the world," she said, kicking her legs back and forth in the air.

"You deserve it."

"Maybe. Maybe not." She pecked me on the lips. "All I want is to be happy with you and my friends." A small laugh escaped her lips. "Becoming a lawyer would be cool too. I can be your sugar mama."

"I have expensive taste." I chuckled and curled my fingers into her sides, tickling her where she was the most sensitive. Somehow, someway, she could always make me smile, even when I felt like shit. "I don't think you'd be able to afford me."

CHAPTER
TWENTY-SIX

ATHENA

"WOULD YOU LIKE ANY SNACKS?" the first-class flight attendant asked, holding a wicker basket of candy, chips, and treats in front of Charlie and me and smiling sweetly.

We were an hour into the flight, and I had been treated like a queen since I'd stepped onto the plane.

I glanced over at Charlie nervously because, usually, in economy, they had the cheap kind of snacks, not these.

To my surprise, Charlie took *two* snacks and looked over at me. "You want any?"

"I'll just take"—I eyed the candy and decided on some M&M's—"these."

"Is that all?" the flight attendant asked.

Did this always happen in first class? They treated me like a totally different person, like I was more important than someone in the back of the economy section who always boarded the flight last. But I mean, they were so nice up here.

"Oh, um …" I grabbed a packet of beef jerky. "I guess this too."

Once I set them on my tray, she moved to the businessmen

behind us. I chewed on the inside of my cheek, looking over at Charlie, who was already staring at me with his darkened eyes. Maybe it was just the lighting here. It was nighttime after all …

I turned back to my laptop to study for the bar exam, which I would take in a couple of weeks. Besides all the drama that had happened lately, I had been studying nonstop for this exam like my life depended on it. I really needed to pass.

After breaking open the M&M's, I popped one into my mouth and peered back over at Charlie, who curled his lips into a smirk. I arched my brow, wondering what he was up to, and pushed an M&M between his lips, hoping that'd make him happy.

When he still didn't look away, I lowered my laptop screen a bit and turned toward him. "Why does it look like you're not up to any good?" I whispered because I knew his smirk all too well. He was up to something.

Charlie finally pulled his gaze away from mine and gestured to his lap.

Or more like the bulge in his pants that he wasn't hiding at all!

Fuck.

Since Charlie had told me that he threw my birth control in the trash this morning, my pussy had been throbbing. I'd had to control myself around him because he was nervous this morning so I didn't want to jump his bones.

But … my panties were soaked, and I was aching for him to be inside me.

I cannot wait to get to the hotel!

"I need your help," he murmured into my ear.

"Charlie," I whisper-yelled at him. "We're tens of thousands of feet in the air!"

He curled a finger around a strand of my red hair and tugged. "Please."

I looked around to make sure nobody was watching. "Charlie, no."

"But you're so pretty," he said, louder than I'd expected. "I can't help it."

After I literally forced myself to turn away from him—because if I didn't, then I would actually reach underneath his tray and start jerking him off—I reopened my laptop and swallowed hard. My nipples were aching to be tugged on inside my bra.

In my peripheral vision, I saw Charlie place a hand on his bulge and squeeze.

Fuck.

Fuck. Fuck. Fuck. Fuck. Fuck. Fuck!

"Please," he whispered, *begging* almost, which was hot as fuck.

My pussy clenched, and I pressed my thighs together. When I didn't respond or start working again, Charlie slipped his hand underneath my blanket and into my pants. I sat up taller, glancing around nervously.

I chewed on the inside of my cheek. "Charlie! What if someone sees us?"

"Oh well."

"Oh well?!"

"Come on, Athie," he whispered into my ear. "Let's get you pregnant."

Warmth exploded through my core, and I clenched hard on his fingers.

He did not just say that with people behind us and the flight attendants just a couple of aisles back!

He pulled his fingers out of me and unbuckled my seat belt without giving me the option of arguing.

"Charlie ..." I whispered.

He wrapped a hand around the front of my throat and pressed his mouth to my ear. "Be a good girl for me and meet me in the restroom. I'll be there in two minutes to fill your cunt with my cum."

My entire body suddenly erupted with tingles. Charlie stood

and stepped into the aisle. I swallowed hard and scooted out of my seat and headed straight for the restrooms up front. The whole plane was about to see us with the restrooms being up here!

After peering back at Charlie, who slid back into his seat, as if he had innocently let me out, I slipped into the crammed restroom and shut—but didn't lock—the door behind me.

God, I can't believe this is happening!

Outside the door, I heard the flight attendant banging around.

Why did I agree to this again? How is Charlie going to get inside without anyone seeing?

This place was so small that I barely fit myself.

Charlie was bigger—I pushed my thighs together—so much bigger.

"More snacks?" the flight attendant asked someone outside the door.

"I'll take a whiskey," Charlie said. "Seat 2B."

"I'll bring it right over," she said, and then someone grabbed the handle.

My heart pounded inside my chest, my pussy absolutely soaked at how wrong this was. We were in public, on a crowded plane, in the middle of the sky! Someone could easily catch us fucking in the restroom.

Charlie stepped into the restroom and shut the door behind us, locking it. Before I knew it, he had me bent at the hip over the small metal sink, his icy eyes on mine in the mirror. He hooked his thumbs into my pants and pulled them down to my mid-thigh.

"The things I've been waiting to do to this pussy," he whispered into my ear, one hand gripping my hair, forcing me to look into the mirror. He pressed his mouth against my soft spot, his stubble tickling my neck. "My balls are filled to the brim with so much cum for you."

I bit down on my lower lip to hold back a whimper. "Charlie …"

He reached into his pants, pulled out his hard cock, and lined it up with my entrance. "I'm going to fuck you so hard that everyone on this plane hears you crying my name, Athie. When you walk out of here, everyone is going to know that your pussy is filled with my kids."

And with that, he slammed into me.

I slapped a hand over my mouth to suppress another moan.

While he barely pulled out of me—there wasn't that much space—he was thrusting into me hard and fast and so goddamn deep. He took one of my tits in his free hand and squeezed my nipple between his forefinger and middle finger.

Another moan left my mouth, this one louder. Pleasure built higher and higher inside my core, and I clenched around him and clutched the sink with all my might. I closed my eyes, feeling his balls slap against my clit with every thrust.

Fuck!

"You're mine, Athie. All mine."

I nodded and continued to squeeze my eyes closed.

He tugged further back on my hair. "Open your eyes and look at me."

After sucking in a sharp breath—the pleasure rising and rising in my core—I opened my eyes and looked at him through the reflection. He drew his nose up the column of my neck, his hooded eyes on mine.

"Beg me," he murmured.

"Please," I whispered.

"Please what?"

"Please, fill me up with your cum," I said, becoming more and more desperate by the moment. My pussy was gripping his cock harder than it ever had, and I was a wet mess. "Please, get me pregnant. Please, make me your wife."

The last plea surprised me—*because how could I say that to him this soon?!*—but a wild groan escaped his mouth, and suddenly, he slammed deep inside me without pulling out. My pussy exploded all around him, and I bit my lower lip hard enough to draw blood.

"Make you my wife," he grunted, pumping into me deeper somehow. "I like the sound of that."

Why did I say that?!

God, the thought of Charlie getting me pregnant felt so good that I wanted to say it again. Make him come inside me over and over.

I continued to ride out my orgasm until he finally pulled out of me. My pussy was stuffed with his cum, and I wasn't going to let any go to waste. Before he had to ask, I pulled up my underwear and pants.

But I didn't want to wait here any longer to talk about what I had just said. The longer we stayed here, the bigger the chance was that we would get caught.

When I opened the restroom door, the attendant glanced over from her station and widened her eyes. Charlie opened the door wider from behind me, still oblivious to the fact that she had caught us.

Or maybe he just didn't care because of what I had said to him.

She opened her mouth to say something to us, but Charlie gently guided me ahead and back to our seats while slipping her some cash. I didn't say a word and sat down in my seat, pulling the blanket over my lap.

Charlie sat beside me. "If you're going to be my wife, then I'll do whatever I can to protect you. Even if that means paying off some flight attendant to keep this quiet."

CHAPTER
TWENTY-SEVEN

CHARLIE

"YOU GONNA BE OKAY HERE?" I asked Athena, glancing out the coffee shop windows and into the casino, where people mindlessly spent their money. It was the only coffee shop in the city that hadn't been absolutely packed this morning and had a place for her to plug in.

Plus, the hotel room was just a block away, so if she needed to head back to the room while I had this meeting, then she should be able to without a problem. I didn't love the thought of leaving her alone in an unfamiliar city, and she had insisted on working in a café.

"I'll be fine," Athena said, plugging her laptop into the wall. "Now, don't be late!"

I placed her iced green tea on the tabletop, then pulled a warmed chocolate croissant out of a bag and set it in front of her. "Make sure you eat so you don't get grumpy. When I get back, I'm going to take you out."

"Good luck!" Athie stood on her toes and pecked me on the lips. "You'll do great."

"I hope so," I murmured against her mouth, then gave her one last kiss.

After peering back at her once more to see her supportive smile, I headed out of the café. One hand around my bag strap that hung off my shoulder and the other stuffed into my pocket, I walked through the casino toward the exit.

It was three in the afternoon, and people were already drunk off their asses while slamming their fingers down on the slot machine or stumbling out of a chapel, hand in hand, snogging each other. I doubted they'd remember this in a few hours.

When I stepped out of the casino, the warm air hit my skin. It was the middle of winter, and California was nothing like Pittsburgh. Though I wasn't sure I enjoyed it here. Being cold gave me an excuse to bundle up with Athie.

I glanced down at my phone and drew my tongue across my lower lip.

A five-minute walk to the building.

If it didn't work out with this venture capital investment, it shouldn't affect me too much. I would still be able to run the company, but it would take a bit longer to get off the ground and really start making money. The investment would help a lot, but it wouldn't be the death of me if I didn't get it.

I walked up the steps and into the bustling building and entered, my mind a mess.

"Do you have an appointment?" the lady at the front desk asked.

"Yes, for Charlie Easton."

The secretary scrolled through her computer, then smiled. "You're just in time. Mr. Harold is waiting for you. Head around the corner, then take the elevator up to the eighteenth floor. The meeting will be in the third room on the left."

"Thanks," I said, clutching my bag strap harder.

The closer I got to this meeting, the more and more I felt like this was the wrong choice.

Chances were that these guys ... were just like Derek. And I didn't want to work with them if they were. I would do anything not to give them a single percent of my company. I didn't need the investment, and I really didn't want to make these guys money in the long-term.

While I had been so caught up in making it work, I had forgotten about the network that I did have. I didn't want to ask any one of my friends for money, but investment and partnerships were different. Everyone benefited from that.

And out of everyone I knew, Michelle—as annoying as she was—would be a great partner.

She already ran two successful businesses—Radiant and her sex toy company—and she had mentioned to me when I was just starting that she would be interested in collaborating with me in some way.

If this didn't work out, screw the investors.

Athie had said she didn't care about the money, and while I knew it to be true, I wanted to give her a really, really great life. I wanted to spoil her and make it so she didn't have to work, if she didn't want to work.

The elevator whizzed up to the eighteenth floor, and suddenly, the doors opened. When I stepped out, the elevator doors to my left opened, too, and out walked Derek fucking Easton with a black eye and a busted lip.

His lips curled into a smirk when he saw me. "Funny seeing you here."

"What the fuck are you doing here?" I asked between gritted teeth.

"Oh, I didn't tell you," Derek said. "I picked up investing in the past few years. I've partnered with Harold to make sure I could get my hands into every last investment that could make me wealthier than you could ever be."

I balled my hands into fists. He had to be lying.

"Fuck you," I snarled under my breath.

"Did you bring Athie along?" he asked. "Bet she's working in a café somewhere."

Restrain yourself, Charlie. Don't fucking hit him.

If he was lying and I hit him here, then coming all the way out here really wasn't worth it. I had convinced Athie to come here with me when she could be back at home with her friends, studying for the bar.

I needed to get something out of this that was *not* being thrown in jail.

"Hey, Derek," a secretary said when we stepped into the lobby.

Derek smirked. "What's up, Sammie?"

"What happened to your face?"

"Ah, don't worry about it," he murmured, glancing at me. "You should see the other guy."

The other guy was about to pummel another fist into his face if he didn't shut the fuck up and stop trying to inject himself into every fucking facet of my life. Didn't he have anything better to do? Of course not.

He didn't have a real job and never applied himself to anything other than my life.

"Right this way," Derek said, guiding me toward the third room on the left, as if it was his first time ever meeting me and he wanted to show the girls up front that he was sweet, caring, and didn't deserve his swollen face.

"What do you want with Athena?" I growled quietly.

"To fuck her." A low chuckle escaped his throat as he grabbed the door handle. "Until she's bloody."

Just as I was about to say something, he pushed the door open, and I plastered a fake smile on my face because I knew this afternoon was about to be shit. I wanted to walk right out of here, but I had come all this way.

All this fucking way just to be shit on by him.

"You must be Charlie," Harold said, firmly shaking my hand. "It's nice to meet you."

"You as well," I said, shaking his hand, then the two other venture capital investors' hands. "Let's get started."

Most importantly, let's get this fucking over with.

ATHENA

"DO you want to talk about it?" I asked Charlie a couple of hours after his meeting.

He hadn't really said much about his meeting since he had met me back at the café in the middle of the casino. While I sat to the left of him at a table at Palate—a really, really expensive restaurant that was way out of my budget—he grabbed my chair leg and pulled me closer to him.

"Not really."

My lips curled into a frown because I loved talking to him, and he didn't seem disappointed, but he was a bit pissed. Thankfully, he had dropped *most* of his annoyance once he picked me up from the café.

"It was a waste of my time," he said, teeth gritted. He blew out a breath and fixed the strap of my pink dress. "Time I could've been working or spending with you."

"Aw," I murmured. "It's not a waste of time to figure out what you don't want to do in life. If you don't want investors or VCs in your business, you don't need to have them. Some businesses do, but I don't think yours does. They'd hinder it anyway."

Charlie's business had a sexual component, and investors loved and hated any business that revolved around sex. They were the biggest hypocrites I had ever witnessed because half of them—as far as I knew—were retired frat boys who cheated on their wives with sex workers or sexualized secretaries.

Sex sells. Except nobody wanted to admit they enjoyed it.

"Sorry for being annoyed on our first real date," he murmured.

"Well," I said, straightening his tie, "why don't we forget all about your meeting?"

"And?"

My lips curled into a smirk. "I was walking around the casino after you left and found—"

"I thought I told you to stay in the café."

I playfully rolled my eyes. "I'm not helpless."

"Someone might have stolen you."

"Oh, believe me, I would not be someone's first choice to steal." I giggled.

He snatched my chin and lifted it. "You'd be my first choice to steal."

"Are you saying that you're a kidnapper?"

A low chuckle left his mouth. "If it was you, yes."

I poked him in the stomach, where I knew he was the most sensitive. "Anyway, as I was saying, I was walking around the casino when you left—*trying to get kidnapped, obviously*—and there's a club opening tonight."

"Where?"

"I think it was between some Mexican restaurant and a chapel. I saw this half-drunk couple who was stumbling nearby with a woman wearing a tux and a man wearing a veil, munching on tacos." I laughed, thinking back to it. "We should go! There was some good dance music playing out front."

"I have something better," he hummed, tugging on a lock of

my red hair that I had curled earlier. "This casino has mini-golf on the third floor. Let's go there first, and then we can get drunk at whichever club you want to dance your pretty little ass off in."

————

"Fuck, you're so hot," Charlie growled against my lips, his drink spilling on the floor.

I danced beside him, one hand around his collar, the other clutching my drink. I forgot how many drinks I had already drunk. Three? Five? Maybe six? Who was counting anymore, honestly? This night had been so fun, especially the mini-golf.

Music thumped through the club. I moved my hips from side to side, grinding my body against Charlie's. We had gone to clubs before, but we always danced around each other, our bodies barely touching. Now, he was mine, and I wasn't going to waste the opportunity.

Plus, with the alcohol running through my veins, I didn't want to stop.

"I wanna bring you to Radiant so badly," he murmured.

Pleasure coursed through my body, and I pressed my thighs together.

Going to Radiant with Charlie?

I had told myself when I went last time that I didn't think I would ever consider going back, and especially not in those glass rooms, but now that Charlie was proposing this idea …

"Oh, yeah?" I asked. "What would you do to me there?"

"Bring you into one of the glass rooms and set up a camera," he said, capturing my bottom lip between his teeth and sucking it into his mouth. "We'll make the glass dark, so we can't see out of them, but everyone can see in. You'll know that they're getting off on you. You'll know that they're watching this sexy body get filled."

I whimpered and ground my thighs together. One of his arms snaked around my waist, and he tugged me closer to him so my tits pressed up against his muscular chest. How he was mine, I honestly didn't know.

"Because you get off almost as much as I do while being watched, don't you?"

After whimpering again, I nodded. "Yes."

"Oh, baby, I know you do," he murmured. "We'll make sure everyone sees you—my online fans, every last member at Radiant, and especially *our friends*. I bet they'd love watching you get fucked by my huge cock."

Fuck!

He took another sip of his drink, and I snagged the straw and sipped some down too.

Charlie had never looked sexier than right now, his gaze all hazy, his mouth mumbling against mine, his needy hands grasping at my hips in front of everyone. He tugged me closer and raked his fingers across my lower back.

Some guy moved closer to us from behind, but he shoved him away while keeping his gaze on me the entire time.

"Let's have one more drink," he murmured.

"One more?"

"Mmhmm."

"And then what?"

He pulled me closer to him until my body was flush against his and his lips were pressed against mine. "Then I'm going to throw you over my shoulder, walk back to our hotel, strip you naked, and fuck you to sleep in front of the windows."

"Fuuuck," I moaned against his lips. "Please."

"I love when you beg for me, Athie," he growled, slipping one knee between my thighs and grinding it up against my cunt.

If he wasn't careful, I would come undone right—

"You sound like a desperate little pet."

Fuck!

I finished my drink and tugged him toward the bar. We'd promised each other one more drink, but I didn't know if I would last that long.

CHAPTER
TWENTY-NINE

ATHENA

MY HEAD THROBBED. I fluttered my eyes open and placed my palm flat against my forehead in hopes that the pain would go away and I could sink back under the blankets with Charlie and waste the day away before we took a red-eye home tonight.

Sunlight blared into the room, only making my headache worse.

Why did I drink so much last night? And how'd we make it back up here?

The last thing I remembered was promising Charlie that we'd have one more drink last night while dancing at that club. After that, I must've blacked out or something because I couldn't remember shit.

Someone knocked on the door. "Room service."

Room service?

I glanced at Charlie, who was still fast asleep, mouth half open and snoring. I hadn't ordered anything, and from what I could tell, Charlie hadn't either. Unless he had forgotten about it and gone back to sleep.

"Mr. and Mrs. Easton?" a female voice said from outside, giving another knock.

Mrs. Easton?

Warm, fuzzy feelings exploded through me, and I slipped out of the bed and grabbed my robe that I had thrown across my suitcase yesterday morning. After tying it around my waist, I padded to the door and looked through the peephole.

A maid stood outside with a cart of trays and coffee.

I unlocked the door and peeked my head out. "Yes?"

"Mrs. Easton, we have the room service that you ordered."

"Oh, um …" I glanced over my shoulder at Charlie, who stirred on the bed, his body shifting underneath the blankets. "We didn't order anything."

"You and your husband ordered late last night at the front desk," she said. "I was told that you wanted it delivered at nine a.m." She opened a notebook and flipped to a page. "Chocolate milk, coffee, a platter of fruit, blueberry and chocolate chip pancakes, and eggs."

"Wow," I whispered. "We must've been hungry."

Or really, really, really drunk.

"Will it be charged to the room?" I asked.

"Yes."

"Okay, I guess we'll take it then."

She moved the cart toward the door, and I took the hint to open it wider. I really didn't want anyone in the room with us, especially with Charlie half naked on the bed. But this should be quick, right?

After placing all the trays and containers onto the dresser, she pushed the cart back toward the door. "The hotel would like to provide you with a complimentary bottle of champagne as well," she said, reaching to the bottom of the cart and pulling out champagne at nine o'clock in the morning. "Congratulations."

"Huh?" I asked, brows furrowed.

Instead of answering, she wheeled out the cart and started

down the hallway. I peered out of the room and stared at her in complete confusion while clutching the bottle.

What the heck is this for?

"Athie?" Charlie mumbled from the bed. "Who was that?"

I twirled around and shut the door behind me, placing the champagne on the dresser. "One of the maids delivering room service that we apparently ordered last night. She also gave us a bottle of champagne. Do you remember ordering anything?"

"I don't remember anything from last night," he murmured against the pillow.

My phone buzzed.

Heather: WHY ARENF'T YOU ANSWERRING!!!!!

Heather: WE NEEF TO KNOW THE DEETS ASAP!!!

My eyes widened at the many, many, many messages that I had received from the group chat. There were at least a hundred of them—half from Heather, misspelling words, and none of them clear about what was going on.

Another message from Sierra.

Sierra: AND THE VIDEO?!

Evelyn: Not sure if you meant to upload it, but it was hooooot.

Oh fuck.

"Hey, Charlie," I whispered, heart pounding so loudly that I could hear it in my ears.

Charlie turned over in the bed, facing me, fluttering open his pretty blue eyes.

My mouth dried. "We didn't happen to record a video last night, did we?"

Charlie shot up straight, eyes wide, and grabbed his phone. "God, I don't remember."

I opened all my social media and thankfully didn't see anything, but I could barely see *anything* with how many more messages kept coming in. One after another after another. Heather. Heather. Heather. Sierra. Heather. Evelyn. Sun. Heather.

More and more group chat notifications popped up, then a direct message from Sun.

Sun: Is it true???

Me: I'm so confused. What happened? I just woke up.

Sun: You don't know?!

Gosh, someone please tell me what's going on!

Me: No!

Sun: Charlie—or someone—posted a video of you guys last night.

Me: Where???

I needed to know so we could get that down ASAP if it was on his social media. I was fine if we were streaming live, but I didn't remember shit about what had happened in whatever video that we must've posted.

"Athena," Charlie said.

As soon as my full name left his mouth, I snapped my gaze to him. He always called me by a nickname unless it was something serious, and by the wide-eyed look he was giving me right now, something had happened.

"What?" I asked, crawling onto the bed next to him to look at his phone.

Oh God, if we uploaded a video when we were both drunk off our asses last night ...

The most I could do was hope that it didn't show either of our faces.

When I looked over his shoulder, there wasn't any video on his screen. I could only see his reflection on the black screen. But Sierra had mentioned a video, and by the way the girls kept blasting up my phone all morning ... there had to be something, right?

"What's going on?" I asked again.

"Do you remember anything about last night?"

"No," I said, grabbing my head. "I drank way too much."

Charlie dropped his gaze to my lap. "Your hand."

"My hand?" I asked, glancing down at them. My eyes widened. "Oh my God."

A diamond sparkled on my left ring finger.

CHAPTER
THIRTY

CHARLIE

"DID WE GET MARRIED?" Athena whispered, staring down at a wedding ring on her finger.

I looked at it, too, in awe—because, damn, I had good taste in jewelry, even when drunk. But also, of course, in complete and utter shock. This couldn't be real, right? There wasn't any place we *could* get married, at least none that I remembered. And definitely not that late last night.

When I had checked the time before our last drink, it had been twelve in the morning.

Eyes shifting from Athena's hand to mine, I spotted a thick black band around my ring finger. I drew the pad of my thumb across it, my heart racing inside my chest.

How could I marry her and not remember a single thing?! What a fool I am.

Athena grabbed my hand to examine it. "We got married."

While I was usually good at reading Athena, I couldn't right now. And that scared the shit out of me. It was soon—really soon—after we had started dating. Hell, last night, we had somehow had our first real date and gotten married, all in one.

My stomach twisted into knots. *What if she regrets it?*

I had to make sure, however she reacted … I didn't scare her away.

"We went to that silly little chapel," Athie said. "It's not real, right?"

Ouch, that hurts. That fucking stings.

"You said you wanted to be my wife," I said, trying to play off her comment.

The words must've come out harsher than I'd expected them to because Athie turned toward me, grabbed my left hand with hers, and intertwined our fingers. "I do, but I wanted it to be special."

Warmth exploded through me, and I tugged Athena into my lap. "I'd say getting married in a casino chapel, drunk off our asses, in the middle of California, is pretty special. Most people plan their weddings."

Athie's unreadable expression suddenly dropped. She slapped my chest, her fingers curling against it, and then she giggled as strands of red hair fell into her face. "I wonder how embarrassing we were. You think we got tacos after?"

"Oh, no doubt. Wouldn't be surprised if you ate one off my ass."

Nose scrunched up, she threw her head back. "Ew! Why would you not be surprised?!"

I curled my fingers into her sides, tickling her right underneath the ribs. She squirmed on top of me and burst out into another fit of giggles. My lips found the base of her neck.

"You're always surprising me with the new kinks you have. Taco kink would be a fine addition."

"I don't know where your ass has been," she said through laughs. "I'm not going near it."

"Wow," I murmured, kissing below her ear and sliding my hands from her waist to her ass. "You're my wife now. You should do anything for me."

"*You* should do anything for me."

"If you asked me to eat tacos off your ass"—I squeezed it in my hands—"I would."

After wiping the happy tears from her cheeks, she set her forearms on my shoulders and stared softly at me for the longest time, her lips curled into a smile. She shyly turned away, letting her hair fall into her face. "What do you think it was like?"

"Our wedding?" I chuckled. "I totally wore the veil."

"I bet," she said. "You'd look good in one."

"I know." My lips curled into a smirk. "You know, that food is probably getting cold."

Athena crawled off me and was about to head for the food before I gently tugged her back down so she could rest. I wasn't going to let her start off the first day as Mrs. Easton by lifting a finger for us.

"No, no, no," I murmured. "Stay in bed, my queen."

After setting down a platter of chocolate chip pancakes with eggs in front of her, I grabbed a plate for myself and plopped down beside her in the bed. My shoulders slumped forward, and I stuffed a forkful of fruit into my mouth.

"So, what about that video?"

"Video?" I asked, eyes widened.

Oh shit. I forgot about that. I was so caught up in her being my wife. My wife!

"Eh, it doesn't matter," I said, shrugging. "Let's look at pictures."

"Charlie!" Athie exclaimed. "I can't find it anywhere on social media."

I shoveled food into my mouth. "Then don't worry about it. It's not like everyone hasn't already seen both of us naked on my stream."

"My friends haven't!"

"Well, there's a first time for everything."

After shooting me a glare, Athena took a bite of her eggs. "Thought you'd want to see our wedding night."

"Wedding night? I want to see the goddamn wedding first!" I

murmured. "It's more important to me than seeing you naked." I wiggled my brows at her. "I can do that anytime I want. Now we have to have pictures, right? We didn't get married and not take any pictures."

"We got married in a dirty casino chapel." She giggled. "I doubt we have anything."

I leaned back against the headboard and opened my phone's gallery. Inside, there were a handful of blurry pictures from the club, after we must've both blacked out. I leaned toward her, showing her my screen.

She rested her forehead against my shoulder and took a bite of her chocolate chip pancakes. "Nuh-uh. We actually took some?" She buried her face into my arm, hiding behind it. "I'm scared."

"Scared, huh?" I hummed, scrolling through to the next set of pictures, where we were in the chapel.

Someone must've taken my phone because we were up at the altar, getting married by a half-naked priest in a sombrero.

"Look at us." I chuckled. "And you said it wasn't special."

"You're right. Not everyone gets married next to a Mexican restaurant."

My lips curled into a smirk, and I let Athie take my phone and start scrolling herself. She drew her lips into a small smile, the sunlight flooding into our hotel room and hitting her pretty eyes, making them a sea of color.

She was so beautiful, and I couldn't believe that she was mine.

Truly mine.

My gaze dropped to our fingers, and warmth spread through my body. We were married.

Married in our early twenties to each other. To my best friend.

Two weeks ago, I would've never guessed that something like this would ever happen. I would've never had the courage to ask her to be mine, to kiss her, to show the love that I'd had for the past few years of my life.

Most of all, I was glad that she was taking this so … lightheartedly.

"What is this?!" she exclaimed, eyes popping out of her head as she scrolled to the next picture. She grasped her stomach and burst out into a fit of laughter. "Oh my God. Oh *my* God."

"I told you that you ate tacos off my ass."

She hid her giggles behind her hand. "At least it wasn't your bare ass."

"What's wrong with my bare ass?"

Instead of responding, she scrolled to the next one, where a drunk Athena and Charlie posed in front of the camera, hugging each other tightly, our hazy eyes half open, and drunken smiles on each of our faces.

"You know," she whispered, dragging her fingers across my jaw, "even if we don't remember it, I'm ecstatic to be married to my best friend in the entire world for the rest of my life, to be Mrs. Easton."

CHAPTER
THIRTY-ONE

ATHENA

"SO, we literally had a half-naked taco enthusiast as our officiant." I giggled, then took a huge bite of my French toast covered with fresh strawberries.

We were at the best place for breakfast and brunch in Pittsburgh.

"Stop," Heather said through chuckles. "You're not serious."

I held my stomach through the belly laughs. "One hundred percent."

Evelyn held out her hand. "We need pictures, or it didn't happen."

After tugging out my phone, I handed it to her. My lock screen was literally the image of Charlie and me being married, surrounded by tacos, burritos, and a half-naked officiant. Why would it be anything different?

The girls passed the phone around, then handed it back to me and laughed over brunch.

"Now, *I'd* like to see that video," I said.

"You mean that you haven't yet?!" Evelyn exclaimed.

My eyes widened. "Should I have?"

Honestly, it should've been the first thing on my mind, but I had been exhausted, and it'd completely slipped my mind. I was overhyped about what had happened at the chapel and all these gushy, gooey feelings.

Sun giggled and leaned toward me, keeping her voice low. "You're literally fucking on the hotel bed with his fingers in your mouth as he tells everyone how you're his wife and the only woman that he's ever loved."

Warmth spread through my body. *Charlie said that?*

I kicked my feet back and forth underneath the table and grinned to myself, taking another bite of my French toast and feeling all tingly. How had it felt, marrying my best friend? I hoped it had been as good as these feelings were.

"Hellooooooo," Sierra said, waving her hand in front of my face. "Earth to Athena."

I shook my head to pull me out of my daydream. "Oh, yeah. You were saying?"

Heather slapped her forehead and giggled. "Oh my God."

"What kind of trance did he put you in?" Evelyn asked, scooping her parfait with a spoon.

"You know, both of your faces are clearly visible," Heather said.

All the gooey feelings dropped. "What?"

"Your face is visible in the video," Sierra said.

"What?!" I exclaimed. "You're not serious."

"That's why we were all so confused that you hadn't watched it yet," Sun said.

"Why didn't you lead with that?!" I said, eyes widening, pulling up Charlie's channel online to search for said video—because while I wanted to watch it, I didn't want my face to be plastered all over the internet.

I have a goal to be a lawyer, for fuck's sake!

"Don't worry; Charlie took it down," Evelyn said. "I tried to watch it again this morning."

"What?!" I asked, brows shooting up. "Again?! Why were you trying to watch it again?!"

Heather giggled. "Come on, Athena. You think we all didn't watch it multiple times? That video was the hottest thing that I had ever witnessed in my entire life. I asked Hector if we could make one when we got married."

My cheeks burned in embarrassment. "Oh. My. God."

When I scanned the table, they all giggled and nodded along in agreement.

"You're telling me that you all watched me naked?" I whispered.

"Yep," Sierra said.

Sun blushed and raised her hands. "I didn't want to, but Heather made me."

"All right, that's a bit of a stretch, Sun," Heather said, sipping on her mimosa. "I sent it to you and said, *Watch this*. I didn't force you to do it! You watched it with your own free will, but I knew your curiosity would get the best of you."

"That's not true!" Sun exclaimed. "You forced me!"

"I did not."

"Heather, yes, you—"

"But didn't you enjoy it?" Heather asked with a smirk.

Sun peeked over at me, cheeks growing even redder.

I sank down in my seat and covered my face with my hands. "Oh. My. God."

As they continued to laugh at my expense, I scooted my seat out and excused myself from the table to take a much-needed pee break in the restroom. My bladder was full with mimosa this morning.

After doing my business, I pushed the restroom door open and smacked right into someone coming out of the men's room. He caught me before I stumbled forward and embarrassed myself even further and set me on my feet.

"Sorry about that, beautiful," he murmured.

My eyes widened, and I glanced up to see a handsome man in his late forties.

While he was fairly attractive, I wasn't into older men, like Sierra, Heather, and Evelyn were. But his playful eyes surely were looking at me like he thought differently. I tucked some hair behind my ear with my left hand so my ring was clearly visible.

"Oh, um …" I said, my cheeks warming. "It's not a problem."

I stared at him for a couple of moments, waiting for him to say something—*anything*—because I was feeling way too awkward right now, but he didn't say a peep. He looked oddly familiar, but I couldn't place it.

"I should get back to my friends," I said, hiking my thumb back toward the restaurant. After stepping back, I twirled around and basically ran back toward the table so he didn't have another chance to talk to me.

When I reached my seat, Heather raised her hand toward the waiter and scribbled in the air, signaling for the check so we could leave. Charlie had said that he had a surprise for me tonight at Radiant, and I wanted to get back home to make myself look nice.

My stomach was doing flips at the thought of him planning stuff for us. He always had, but it felt different now that we were married. A giggle escaped my throat. I still couldn't get over the fact that handsome man was my husband!

It had been on my mind nonstop since we had returned from Cali last night. I hadn't even been able to study for the bar exam on the plane because I couldn't stop staring at how the diamond sparkled on my left hand.

The waiter walked over with a smile. "You ladies are all set."

"What about the check?" Sierra asked, brows drawn together.

"It's all paid for," he said.

"By who?" Evelyn asked, looking around. "You think the guys are here?"

After I scanned the restaurant, the waiter placed the black check presenter in front of me. He smiled and walked away to assist another customer. I arched a brow and opened it up in front of the girls, spotting a scribble for a signature and a note in black ink.

Your husband's a lucky man, stranger. ;)

CHAPTER
THIRTY-TWO

CHARLIE

WIND SEARED MY CHEEKS. *Ah, back to the wonderful winter in Pittsburgh.*

I tugged my hood over my head and walked to the entrance of Radiant while staring down at my phone, buzzing with the name *Mom*.

When I reached the entrance, I walked through the first set of doors and shook off the snow. Mom's call went to voicemail. I clicked on the message and placed the phone up to my ear to get this over with.

"Hi, sweetheart. It's Mom," Mom said on voicemail. "I heard that you got married over the weekend, and your father and I are terribly sad that you didn't tell us about it. We would have thrown you a huge party instead of you having some wedding at a dirty casino chapel. Call me back."

I deleted her voicemail and scrolled to the next one.

"Son," Dad said on voicemail, "give me a call. We need to talk. It's about the party."

No, thank you. Delete.

Not sure what the fuck he wanted to talk about, but I didn't want to entertain it. I'd promised them I'd attend one more party with Athena, and then that was it. No calls. No texts. I didn't want any part in talking to them.

Honestly, I didn't even want to do that because I didn't want Athena to meet them. But she was now my wife, and I wanted to show her off to everyone to prove to them that I didn't need their money to be happy.

Or maybe it was just to prove to myself, especially after that failed money-raising round.

After stuffing my phone into my suit pocket, I shrugged off my coat and handed it to Winter, the coatroom attendant. She tucked some brown hair behind her ear and blushed in a way that she rarely ever did around me.

"Michelle here?" I asked, brushing it off.

She grinned at me. "Last I saw her, she was at the bar with Hector and Steven."

"Thanks."

"No problem," she said, rocking forward. "Let me know if you need anything, Charlie."

While walking toward the main room, I gave her a side-eye. *Weird.*

"There he is," Steven said, sipping on his drink when I walked in. "How'd it go in Cali?"

"Listen," I said, waving them off, "I really don't want to talk about it."

"Come on," Steven said, squeezing my shoulder as I sat. "Didn't smooth-talk them?"

"My brother was there." I nodded to Abdul. "My regular, please."

Hector shook his head in disappointment. "So, you didn't get the deal?"

"When I saw him there, I didn't want the fucking deal," I growled.

"He's like a gnat, isn't he?"

"Hey, Charlie," Samantha, a regular at Radiant, murmured, dragging her fingers across my shoulders.

I offered her a nod. "Hey, what's up?"

"He's taken," Michelle said, walking up to me and twisting me away with her grip on my upper arm. When she finally turned away, Michelle slapped me upside the head. "Stupid boy."

Abdul handed me my drink.

"What did I do?" I asked.

"You're oblivious."

"Oblivious to what?"

Michelle slipped on a stool beside Hector, sharing a look with her brothers, which meant that they all knew something that I apparently didn't. It wasn't unusual for me to greet people who attended Radiant, was it?

"What?" I asked, brows furrowed.

"You have a wedding band on your left hand," Steven noted.

I glanced from Steven to Hector and Michelle, who nodded in agreement. "And?"

"And some women like to take that as a challenge," Michelle said. "In my opinion, I think it's gross, but if you're here alone and without Athena, then girls like that are going to flirt with you to see if they can get with you."

"Why?" I asked, scrunching my nose. "I'm not interested."

"Doesn't matter," Hector said. "They will."

"Does it happen to both of you?" I asked Hector and Steven.

"I really only ever come here with Sierra," Steven said. "And when I don't, it's with him."

Hector nodded to Michelle. "And Michelle doesn't leave me when I'm here alone, so I don't see that type of flirting much anymore. *Thank God.* But if I didn't own this place, Heather would probably be in jail for how possessive she's become over me." He smiled. "I like it."

I gulped. Athena was more insecure than possessive. She wouldn't hit anyone, but she'd hold it all in and not tell me that something was bothering her until it was way too late. It hadn't happened before we started dating, but maybe I had never noticed it.

"You have one of two options," Michelle said, holding up two fingers. "Either you don't come here without Athena or make it a thousand percent clear that you're off the market and you don't entertain anyone, not even with a smile."

"What about Athena?" I asked. "She has a ring on her finger."

"It doesn't happen as much with women," Steven said.

Michelle raised a brow. "Is that what you think? She's pretty. People will hit on her either way. The last wedding I attended with my ex, an older gentleman came up to us with his wife and told my ex that I was way out of my ex's league. It will happen."

"It's not Athena that you have to worry about," Hector said.

Oh, believe me, I knew that with Derek. I trusted Athena one hundred fucking percent, but I wasn't sure she trusted me as much. I had more experience than her in the bedroom, and there were hundreds of videos of me floating around the internet with other women.

I couldn't even let her think I had something with another woman.

Michelle was right. Either I came here only with Athena or not at all.

"You'd best be careful, Easton," Michelle hummed. "I wouldn't be surprised if Nadia came back and started trouble between you and the missus. Girls like her are delusional and will do anything to win."

I set my drink down. "So will Derek."

He was probably the biggest threat that I had to worry about around Athena.

"True. Well, I'm off, boys," Michelle called over her shoulder. "I have a hot date tonight. Have fun!"

"Wait, hold up," I said, jumping off my seat. "You have some time to talk this weekend?"

Michelle raised her brow. "About?"

"Collaborating."

"On?"

"Business."

A smile crossed her face. "Business with Charlie Easton? Count me in."

CHAPTER
THIRTY-THREE

CHARLIE

WITH TWO SLICES of cheesecake from Doughburgh in one hand and a bottle of wine tucked underneath my arm, I unlocked our apartment door and walked into the room. Soft music played over our living room speaker, but Athena wasn't around.

"Athie," I hummed. "Where are you?"

"In here!" she called from the hallway.

I placed the cheesecake on the living room table and headed to the kitchen to find us wineglasses. While I planned to bring Athena to Radiant tonight for our first night together there, foreplay was a must.

What better foreplay than to watch the video we made after marrying?

On the kitchen counter, Athena had laid out several candles with drying wax, which looked like she had made less than an hour ago. My lips curled into a smile, and I popped open the wine to begin pouring.

"Athie, I know you want to watch our video," I called.

Quick footsteps pattered down the hallway, and Athena

popped her head around the kitchen door. Her red hair was thrown up into a messy bun, and she wore an oversize pink-and-white striped shirt.

"You have the video?" she asked, eyes growing wide.

"Yes." My lips curled into a smirk. "Do you want to see it?"

She walked into the kitchen until she stood in front of me, and then she craned her head up and nodded. "Yes, I would like to see it very much. The girls have already seen it multiple times and kept making jokes about it all day! Have you seen it yet?"

"No." I drew my thumb across her lower lip. "I wanted to wait for you."

Her cheeks reddened. "Really?"

"Really."

A giggle escaped her lips. "And you brought wine and ..." She sniffed and glanced at the living room coffee table. "Cheesecake from Doughburgh?!" She grinned and stood on her toes to kiss me on the lips. "Give me five minutes so I can slip into something more comfortable."

When she turned to run to her bedroom, I grabbed her wrist and pulled her back toward me. "I have something for you to wear tonight. It's in my bedroom closet. Second drawer from the top in the bureau. You're to wear it to Radiant."

"Radiant?" she repeated. "We're going there tonight?"

"Yes."

My gaze dropped to Athena's thighs as she discreetly tried to push them together. Her nipples hardened under her oversize shirt. I placed the wine down and seized them to pull her closer to me.

"You're going to put it on for me, and then we'll watch our sex tape. Then I'll bring you to Radiant to show off this pretty little body," I mumbled against her lips. "Do you understand me, Athie? You're going to be my willing little cum dumpster in front of all your friends."

Athena whimpered and swallowed hard. "Yes ... please."

Once I released her nipples, I twirled her around and

smacked her ass. She jumped in the air and giggled, skipping into the hallway.

I finished pouring the wine and glanced over my shoulder. "Oh, and, Athie?"

"Mmhmm?"

"We're married. We're not going to sleep in separate rooms anymore," I said. "So, after Radiant tonight, I'll move your stuff into my bedroom. Got it?"

"Yep, I under—" she said, her voice becoming more distant. "Charlie!"

My lips curled into a smirk. She had found her lingerie for tonight.

"Why is it so small?!" she exclaimed. "It doesn't even cover my nipples or pussy. There is literally a slit right down the middle. You expect me to wear this to Radiant?! Won't everyone look at me?"

"That's the point," I murmured.

"Charlie!"

"Don't make me come in there and put it on you."

"But—"

"Athena …"

"Give me a sec! It's literally just strings. I don't know what goes where!"

I grabbed the wineglasses and headed to the living room. "You have two minutes."

As I set down the glasses and pulled out the cheesecake, I listened to curse words and a loud thump, followed by another curse, then my closet door shutting. I peered into the hallway and opened up the cheesecake for Athena.

"One minute," I warned.

Then I connected my phone with the television, pulling up the video and pausing it right in the beginning so we could watch it from the start. It was twenty minutes long, and all Athena wore in the thumbnail were white heels and a veil.

My dick hardened inside my pants, and I couldn't fucking wait for this.

A moment later, Athena peered with just her head from the hallway. "Okay, I think I figured it out." She covered her face with her hand to hide a blush. "Don't make fun of me though. I don't know how good it looks on me."

I sat down in the chair across from the couch and stared at her, crooking my finger. "Have I ever made fun of you? That's not something a good husband would do, Athie. Now, come here before I make you."

She shuffled out of the bedroom and into the hallway, covering her stomach with her hands. "Really, I'm not sure if—"

"Fuck, you look so sexy," I murmured, pressing my hand against my dick inside my pants. My cock throbbed at the sight of her. I couldn't wait until I got her pregnant. "I so fucking excited to show you off to everyone tonight."

Athena entered the living room, sat down on the couch, and pulled a pillow onto her lap to hide her body from me. Sure, this wasn't Athena's style in lingerie, but my wife wasn't going to hide her body from me.

I moved from the chair to sit beside her on the couch, threw her pillow across the floor, and captured her chin in my hand to kiss her on the mouth. "Don't hide yourself from me, Athie. You're mine."

Once I released her, I grabbed some cheesecake on a fork and fed her. Her tense smile softened, and she closed her eyes, moaning. Doughburgh was her favorite. I took a bite of the cheesecake myself, then gave her another. Her shoulders rolled forward, and she leaned against me, completely relaxed.

"I'm going to turn on the video now," I said. "Okay?"

She finished chewing, swallowed, then picked up her wine. "Okay."

I pressed Play on the screen. On the television, the video began playing, and the camera was moving wildly on the bed that we must've posted it on as I thrust into her from behind her.

One of my hands was wrapped around Athena's throat, the other playing with her pussy.

It hadn't even been thirty seconds, and Athena's moans from the video were already making pre-cum dribble out of my hard cock inside my pants. And her dirty talk …

Fuck, it is better than mine. Where'd that come from?

No wonder why it had been viewed thirty thousand times before I took it down.

On the couch beside me, Athena ground her thighs together. "Charlie …" Her nipples were hard, and she swallowed down a sip of wine. "I don't think I can wait until we get to Radiant tonight."

THIRTY-FOUR

ATHENA

"YOU MEAN ... when I get inside, I'm going to have to *take off* this coat?" I asked Charlie, tugging the white fur coat that he had bought me last year for Christmas closer to my body. Underneath, I only had on the slinky lingerie.

Which basically meant I was wearing *nothing*.

It was all strings with very little lace that barely covered anything.

Charlie intertwined his fingers with mine. "Yes."

My cheeks reddened from embarrassment and the harsh Pittsburgh wind. I swallowed nervously and slowed down on the sidewalk, spotting the door to Radiant less than half a block away.

All my friends were here tonight with their lovers, and by the way that they had kept poking fun at me today over brunch, I didn't doubt that they would watch if Charlie invited them to. And if we were going in one of those glass rooms, I didn't really have a choice.

Heat warmed between my thighs. I mean, it was kinda ... hot.

But at the same time, so, so, so embarrassing! These were my best friends.

"What are you worried about?" Charlie asked, squeezing my hand. The wind whipped his white-blond hair into his face against his chiseled features, and I couldn't believe he was mine. "You're going to be the hottest one there."

My mind wandered to Nadia. I hoped that we wouldn't see her here tonight. I honestly didn't know what I would do if she showed up halfway through Charlie fucking me over one of those beds. I'd be so thrown off that I didn't think I'd be able to finish.

When we reached the doors, Charlie opened it for me. My stomach twisted into knots, and I reluctantly entered the building.

How the heck am I supposed to get naked and fucked here? I'm nervous, just walking into this place.

After capturing my hand, Charlie led me through the second set of doors. A waft of vanilla drifted through my nose as we walked to the coatroom, where an attendant bounced on her toes behind the counter.

"Nice to see you again today, Charlie," the attendant said.

She smiled extra long at Charlie, batting her lashes. Jealousy pooled in my stomach, but when Charlie didn't even look back at her, it disappeared. He hadn't taken his eyes off me since we had left his car.

"Take off your coat, Athena," Charlie said, leaning against the counter with a smirk.

Heart pounding so loud that I could hear it in my ears, I swallowed hard and slowly unzipped the jacket. As soon as the zipper reached below my small breasts, my nipples hardened from the sudden coldness.

"Charlie …" I whispered. "Are you sure this is okay?"

Of course it was, but I was scared of what people would say about me. People walked around Radiant completely naked, but they had billion-dollar bodies. And my small boobs didn't compare to any of them. Not even my friends.

Charlie pushed himself off the counter, stalked toward me, and grabbed the zipper that was halfway down my chest. I swallowed hard and released it, letting him take control. Music thumped out from the main room, but I could barely hear it over my racing heart.

When Charlie fully unzipped me, he tugged the coat off my shoulders, and I stood in the middle of the lobby, practically naked. Wetness pooled between my thighs, my nipples hard and aching to be pulled.

"There you go," he murmured against my lips, taking my hand. After placing a kiss on my lips, Charlie turned to the woman behind the counter and handed her my coat. "Tell my wife how sexy she looks."

"Charlie!" I scolded quietly, burying my face into the crook of his arm.

To my surprise, she offered me a smile. "You look great, Mrs. Easton."

Charlie then led me into the big room, where a crowd of people chatted, danced, drank, and fucked all around us. I hid behind his shoulder, in hopes that everyone would turn around and mind their business, but if I really wanted that, then I would've stayed home. I had willingly come with Charlie and agreed to wear this lingerie for him.

"Don't be a brat with me, Mrs. Easton," he growled, turning around in front of me and taking a step back so I wasn't covered by him at all. He captured my nipples between his fingers and tugged on them. "We're going to see your friends."

"Okay, okay, but can you release me first?" I said, cheeks burning.

"No."

Instead, Charlie continued to move backward while pulling me along by my nipples. I whimpered because everyone was now really staring, but my pussy was warm, tight, and soaking wet.

In the crowd of people, I spotted Sierra, Heather, Steven, and Hector at the bar.

"Oh no." Sierra giggled, nudging Heather as we approached. "Someone's in trouble."

Heather peered over her shoulder, along with Steven and Hector. "Damn!"

Oh God.

"Look at you!" she shouted, jumping off the barstool.

Sierra laughed behind her hand.

"No, please, don't look at me," I said as Charlie squeezed harder to pull me along.

So embarrassing …

But my pussy was pulsing.

"Sun," Heather shouted halfway across the room at Sun.

Sun was perched on Russ's lap with his wife on his opposite leg.

Heather waved her arms in the air to get her attention. "Athena's here."

"Oh my God," I murmured to myself, keeping my gaze on Charlie.

If I pretended like nobody else was here, then it'd be like we were live on Charlie's profile. Charlie's icy eyes were piercing into mine.

He sat down beside Hector and leaned against the bar. "Are you going to behave?"

"Mmhmm," I whimpered.

Once he finally released me, he seized my chin and kissed me. "You're so pretty."

Another whimper left my mouth, and I kept my eyes closed for a moment. Music drifted through my ears, and my heart was racing faster than it ever had. But Charlie's hands were on my body, calming me.

"I ought to collar you next," he murmured into my ear. "Would you like that?"

"Collar me?" I whispered, warmth exploding through my pussy. "Yes."

Sierra and Heather had both been collared, and I was a bit jealous about it. But that was way before Charlie and I got together. I had wanted it so badly with him, but I never thought that it would happen.

"Your usual?" the bartender said behind the counter.

Charlie nodded.

"And for the pretty lady?" he asked, gazing toward me.

"Tequila," I said without hesitation.

"Tequila?" Charlie repeated with a chuckle.

My lips curled into a small smile. "I need something strong."

When the bartender slipped me my shot of alcohol, I drank it down in one huge gulp and let it burn the back of my throat. Charlie sipped his drink and stood up.

"Well …" he said to our friends. "We're off to the glass room. Feel free to come watch."

"Oh, we will," Heather said, wiggling her brows at me.

And with that, Charlie led me out of the room and down the hallway toward all the glass rooms. My heart was pounding quickly inside my chest at the thought of … people watching us. Not behind a screen anymore. But live.

Some people lingered in the hallway, making themselves known on the couches. I sucked in a breath, my nipples hardening. We had done this more than once now, but all online. Nothing like … this.

Charlie found an empty room and pushed a key into the lock.

"Come on, *wife*," Charlie murmured into my ear. "Let's give them a show."

THIRTY-FIVE

ATHENA

WHEN I STEPPED into the room, vanilla drifted through my nostrils. I inhaled the sweet scent and slightly relaxed my shoulders. Charlie shut and locked the door behind us, then adjusted the glass walls to be completely transparent both ways.

My heart pounded in my ears as my gaze drifted to the bed.

The bed where Charlie would ... fuck me in front of everyone.

Once Charlie placed the key on a small table near the door, he turned toward me while unbuttoning his dress shirt. Warmth gathered between my thighs, my nipples hardening. Still, I couldn't believe that this was happening.

Charlie and I are really going to fuck in front of everyone.

After my husband tugged off his shirt, he walked to another table that had two glasses and some whiskey on the counter. He poured one glass, then walked to the bed where I sat.

He placed his hand on my throat. "Open your mouth."

Excitement rushed through me, and I stared up at him and opened my mouth.

This is really happening!

Charlie sipped the whiskey, but instead of drinking it down, he kissed me on the mouth and gave it to me. I swallowed it in one sip, his hand drifting from my throat down to my pussy. He drew his finger around the string of my lingerie, then slid it between my folds.

"You're so wet for me already, *wife*," he murmured against my mouth.

Almost instinctively, I spread my legs and nodded up at him.

He drifted his fingers across my chin to my lips. "Keep your mouth open."

I reopened my mouth and stuck out my tongue. Charlie took another sip and swished it into his mouth, then placed down the cup. He wrapped his hand around the front of my throat.

This time, instead of kissing me, he spit the drink into my mouth.

Warmth exploded through my body, and I pressed my thighs together. *Fuck!*

"Spit on me again," I panted after drinking down the whiskey. I reached for his hard cock in his suit pants and stroked him through his pants, desperate for all of him tonight and slowly relaxing in front of everyone. "Please …"

After pulling his cock out of his pants, he gripped it in his veiny hand and took another sip of the whiskey. He placed the head of his cock on my tongue. "Show me how badly you want it, *wife*."

God, he knows exactly what he's doing, calling me that!

I wrapped my lips around the head of his cock and sucked him into my mouth, eyes up on his. I moved closer to him and took more and more of his huge cock into my mouth until he hit the back of my throat.

Even then, I didn't stop.

Spit and drool rolled down my chin, my eyes watering. I stared up at him through the tears and gagged, desperate for him to spit in my mouth again, desperate for him to fuck me, to show the world that I truly was his wife.

That he owned me now.

When I pleased him enough, he pulled out of me. Then he rubbed my spit all over my face, ruining my makeup that I had done before we left. I stuck out my tongue, desperate for more, pleading and begging with my eyes.

"More, more," I begged. "Please, more!"

He spit the drink into my mouth once more, then climbed up onto the bed with me, his mouth on mine and one of his hands between my legs. "Tell me what you want me to do to this fuck-able pussy."

"Tell you?" I whispered, glancing over at the glass windows. "But it's embarrassing."

What if I say something wrong and everyone laughs while watching us?

"It's just you and me, baby," Charlie murmured against my lips so quietly that nobody would be able to hear us, his icy gaze on mine. "You're talking to *me*. Not to them. Tell me what you want me to do to you."

Another whimper left my mouth, and I drew my thighs together as best as I could, the pressure building in my core becoming unbearable. "Charlie ..." My cheeks warmed, my heart racing even harder.

"You and me, baby. That's all. It's just you and me."

"Fuck me hard," I cried, hating all this teasing. "Please, shove your big dick into my tight little pussy." I spread my legs and stared up at him, letting him see how my pussy kept clenching at the thought of him being inside me. I gently took his chin in my hand. "Take it all."

"Athena," Charlie growled, quite gutturally, taking his cock in one hand and placing it against my entrance. Pre-cum drooled out of it, and he used his head to rub it all over my entrance and clit, making it glisten. "Look what you do to me."

"Give it to me. Please give it to me," I whimpered and pulled him closer. "I know you want to fill up my tight, breedable little hole."

Charlie's gaze wavered, and it looked like he was losing control, like just by this silly embarrassing dirty talk in front of everyone, he couldn't take it. Charlie kissed me hard on the mouth and shoved himself deep into me.

I cried out in pleasure, my eyes rolling back in my head.

"Is this how you want it?" he growled into my mouth.

"Deeper!" I cried, sinking my nails into his shoulders. "Faster! Harder! More!"

Charlie savagely thrust into me, his hands coming around my waist, pumping into me over and over and over, each time getting deeper, going faster, harder. Giving me more, just as I'd asked.

While I tried to say more words to him, I couldn't get them past my lips. My entire body was trembling from the mere force that he had, using my body for his pleasure. I sank my nails into his muscle, scratching down his back.

"If you're not drawing blood with those pretty claws, I'm not fucking you hard enough."

Before I could get a word out of my mouth, he crawled further up the bed, pushing me to the headboard like a wild animal, thrusting in and out of me more savagely than he ever had. Charlie Easton definitely knew how to put on a show.

"I'm your dirty little whore," I cried. "I'm Charlie's dirty little whore!"

"My dirty little whore," Charlie growled. "And my wife."

Pressure rose higher inside me, and I gripped on to him as hard as I could because I was moments from … moments from … losing all control and … and … I threw my head back and dragged my nails down his back.

"Oh my God!" I screamed, my legs trembling.

I shoved my heels into the mattress and tried to scramble back because the pressure was way too much for me to handle, but Charlie grabbed me and held me close the entire time, not pulling out of me once.

"Fuck, baby," he murmured, kissing on my neck. "I love the way your pussy grips on to my dick when you come."

"Charlie!" I cried, breathing heavily.

He twirled us over so I lay on my stomach and tugged my hips up into the air. After positioning himself at my entrance from behind, he wrapped his hands around the front of my mouth, like his hands were a muzzle on me, and plunged deep inside me. I curled my toes and cried out in pleasure.

"More. More. More. More! Fuck me harder!" I cried.

While I wasn't purposefully putting on a show and I didn't feel any need to, I couldn't get over the exhilaration of people watching us fuck in real life. Sure, on the internet was great, but this ... God, it was phenomenal.

I wanted to fuck like this all the time.

Charlie released his grip on my chin and shoved my upper body into the mattress. My hips were way up in the air, my back arched hard. I gazed back at him, my eyes rolling back into my head at the pleasure.

"Fucking show them how tight this pussy is," he growled.

He turned on the bed so I wasn't facing toward the main glass wall anymore. Instead, everyone watching outside could see us from the side. Charlie grasped my left hip and pulled out of me slowly, watching the way my pussy clenched hard on to him.

"Fuck, baby," he murmured. "This is a desperate, fuckable, *breedable* pussy."

I tightened even more at the thought of Charlie breeding me in front of everyone.

"Do you like when they watch?"

"Mmhmm ..."

"Words, baby. Use your words."

"I love it," I cried. "I love it so, so much!"

CHAPTER
THIRTY-SIX

CHARLIE

ONCE ATHENA FINISHED, I set her down on the bed and stood to fog the glass room walls. I enjoyed when people watched us, and it seemed like Athena did, too, but I wanted to give her proper aftercare, which I hadn't done much of lately. It didn't need to be on display for everyone.

After I lay on the bed, Athena crawled into my lap and curled up into me. I gently drew my fingers through her hair and kissed her forehead, rocking us back and forth slightly. Her breathing evened out, and she quickly was fast asleep in my arms.

"I love you," I whispered into Athie's red hair.

I lay back against the headrest and smiled to myself, unable to wait to bring her home and eat that cheesecake with her as she finished pouring her candles. Butterflies fluttered in my stomach, and I couldn't believe that this was my life.

When I had grown up around Derek and my father … all they wanted from women was sex.

It felt nice to look forward to something else, something more intimate.

Had I outgrown that stage already? Dad and Derek were still

in it. Yet, somehow, I wanted nothing to do with sex with strangers anymore. I wanted one woman, and I would be spending my life with her forever.

Coming home to Athena. Having a family with Athena. Growing old with Athena.

I couldn't imagine myself with anyone else, and I didn't want to even think about either of us with someone else. But based on what Hector and Steven had told me earlier, other people would rather stick their nose in everyone else's business.

"I'm tired," Athena murmured in her sleep.

"Sleep, my love," I said, placing her down on the mattress and pulling up the blankets.

Once I cleaned up, I'd bring her home, but I didn't want to leave this place a mess for Michelle and the cleaners to tidy up. So, I pulled on my clothes, walked to the door, and turned off the light so she could get some sleep.

After stepping out, I locked the door and slipped the key into my pocket. Radiant was safe, but I didn't trust just anyone here. I couldn't leave Athena alone in one of these rooms with the door unlocked.

I headed to the back hallway, but had to walk through the main room first.

"Poor performance in there," someone said behind me.

I turned my head and stared at my father, who sat at the bar, drawing his finger around the rim of his glass with his eyes focused on mine, a smirk within them. I pressed my lips together and tried not to let him get to me.

"What are you doing here?" I asked nonchalantly.

But what the fuck is he doing here? In Pittsburgh, out of all the places he could be in the fucking world?! Not New York City or LA or Europe. Here in Pittsburgh, in the freezing fucking cold, all to what? See me?

"Why haven't you answered any of my texts or calls?" he asked.

"I've been busy."

"Busy getting married?"

"Busy traveling for work," I said, wanting to keep Athena out of this as much as I could.

Dad was here for a reason, and I really hoped that reason wasn't her. He definitely knew about her, and he'd probably already had one of his assistants write up an entire file on her. She didn't fit the Easton name or family. Not to my parents' standards.

"Athena …" Dad said. "Is that her name?"

I gritted my teeth. "What do you want?"

Dad called to Abdul, who had been listening, but not looked over yet. Abdul peered at me, then at my father, who nodded to the bottle of whiskey behind him.

"Get my son one. He needs it."

"Actually, I'm going home right now."

"You're really going to wake your wife, all because you don't want to talk to me?" He took another sip and shook his head in disappointment. "I thought I'd taught you better than that, son. Women need their beauty sleep."

God, I fucking hate him.

He gestured to the seat beside him. "Sit down."

After blowing a breath through my nose, I nodded to Abdul for my regular and sat down in the stool next to my father, not sparing him a second glance. "I'll tell you what I told Derek. One more party, and then I'm done with this family."

Dad chuckled. "Is that so?"

Abdul slid my drink across the bar, and I nodded. "Yes."

"What're you going to do about your expenses? Your little business?" he asked.

"Why do you care?" I hissed. *It's not like you ever have before.*

"You think your wife wants to be poor? Not when all her friends are with billionaires."

I bit my tongue. *How the fuck does he know so much about her already?* Besides, Athena wasn't like Mom, nor was she like any of the girls that Derek brought home to meet them.

"Athena doesn't care about that," I said.

"Sure."

I grabbed the glass tightly. "She doesn't."

"She sure seemed happy when I took care of their bill at brunch today," he said.

My nostrils flared, and I snapped my gaze over at him. "What?"

His lips curled into a smirk. "You heard me."

Athena and the girls had seen him at brunch today? She hadn't told me that. Usually, she came bouncing back into the apartment after someone complimented her or paid for her coffee. To pay for an entire brunch and for her not to say anything …

Maybe she had forgotten.

"We're not going to be living in poverty," I said. "You don't know what poverty is."

"Maybe not, but *love*"—the word came out in a chuckle—"if that's what this is, can only go so far."

I gulped down my drink in two more sips to ease the fury building inside me right now. He was trying to get under my skin, and he was succeeding. I fucking hated the mind games that he had been playing with me since I had been a child.

"She's a cute girl," Dad said. "Blushing and everything in the restroom."

He's lying. He's fucking lying.

"What were you doing in the restroom with her?" I asked, seething.

After another chuckle, he set his glass down on the counter, squeezed my shoulder, and walked right out of the room without another word.

CHAPTER
THIRTY-SEVEN

CHARLIE

AS SOON AS my father stepped out of the room, I shot up in my seat and made a beeline for the glass room where I had left Athena. Something wasn't right about what he had said, nor could I figure out why he had said it.

Paying for her meal? Slipping into the restroom with her? Was he trying to impress her?

While I knew he had never been faithful to my mother, Athena wasn't his type. Did my entire family just have something against me being fucking happy? Did they want to see me rot, just like them? Well, too fucking bad.

After unlocking the door, I stepped into the room and spotted Athena on the bed, how I had left her, except now she was awake. I scanned the rest of the room for any sign of that fucker because I didn't trust him.

"Where'd you run off to?" Athena asked from the bed, her red hair wild, like she had just been thoroughly fucked and was well rested. She pulled the blankets up to her chin, her eyes hazy, the way they always were when her pussy was wet.

Growling, I closed and locked the door behind me. "Do you want to go home?"

"Why? Do you?"

"Do you want to go home, Athena?"

When I said her name, she widened her eyes. "No …"

I tugged off my shirt and changed the glass so everyone outside could see into the room. "Good, because I'm going to make you come until you can't stand."

Athena sat up in the bed. "Charlie—ah!"

I snatched up her ankle from underneath the blankets and tugged her to the very edge of the bed, and then I ripped the covers off her so everyone at Radiant could see how lucky I was that Athena was mine.

While my father had walked out of the room during our conversation, I'd bet that he hadn't left Radiant yet. He was still here, lurking, waiting to get Athena alone. And I wasn't sure if he would try to pay her off or sleep with her himself by the way he had acted.

So, I planned to show him who she belonged to … *me*.

"W-wasn't earlier enough—" Athena started. "Oh God!"

After I pressed my mouth against her pussy, she arched her back and tugged on my hair. I flicked my tongue against her clit repeatedly and pushed two fingers into that tight little hole. Athena's legs jerked up.

"Charlie!" she cried.

"That's fucking right. Scream my name, baby."

Her pussy clamped down on my fingers, and suddenly, she made a mess on them. She dug her heels into the mattress as an orgasm exploded through her, desperately trying to squirm away. But I wasn't going to let her go anywhere.

I wrapped my hand around her throat and pinned her to the mattress.

"Charlie," she whimpered, pushing my head away. "Charlie, it's too much pressure!"

My lips wrapped around her clit, and I sucked, my gaze on

her face. I pushed my fingers into her, finding her G-spot and massaging it over and over. She arched her back again, her cunt wrapping tightly around me.

She was going to come again. And again. And again. And again.

I didn't care how long it took. I'd make sure that fucker knew Athena wasn't going anywhere with him. Athena was mine. Only *I* could make her feel this good. Only *I* could give her this pleasure.

He wanted to talk about me not being enough for Athena? Well, an old prick like him wasn't going to last this long with her. So, he could shut his fucking mouth and watch me please my wife.

Athena grabbed the blankets in her fists and yanked up on them, exploding around me again. And still, I didn't pull my mouth away. I began pumping my fingers into her this time, my other hand traveling from her neck to her nipples and squeezing.

"Oh my fucking God!" she screamed. "Oh my fucking God! Oh my fucking God!"

Another orgasm.

Then another.

And another.

When Athena's body didn't stop trembling, I flipped her onto her stomach so she was facing the glass walls, and then I crawled on top of her from behind, one hand around her throat and the other gently caressing her body.

"Charlie," she whimpered. "Charlie, it's too much."

"Do you feel good?" I murmured against her neck.

She pressed her thighs together and nodded.

So, I snaked my arm around her waist and dipped my hand between her legs, fondling her pussy once more. I ground my hard cock against her ass, getting myself off too from the sight of my wife coming more times than I could count.

"You didn't tell me that someone paid for your brunch this morning," I said into her ear.

"Huh?" she asked in a haze.

"You didn't tell me someone paid for your brunch this morning."

She laid her cheek on the mattress and gazed back at me. "I must've forgotten. Is that what this … is about?"

"No, this is about the man who paid; he was my father."

Athena widened her eyes. "Charlie, I didn't—"

"He said that you were in the restroom with him."

"What?!" she exclaimed. "I was not. I bumped into him while exiting the—"

"I know; I know," I said, kissing her shoulder.

"Charlie, I promise that nothing happened."

"I know that you wouldn't betray me." I placed another kiss on her neck. "I trust you."

I tugged up on her hair so her upper body was pressed against the mattress but everyone outside could see my wife's pretty face. And behold, the man of the hour, my own father, stood front and center, watching us.

I rubbed her clit in small circles, sucking on her skin. "Tell everyone who owns you."

"You do," she said between moans. "You do. You do. You do! You do!"

"Louder," I growled. "I want everyone to know before we leave Radiant tonight."

"Charlie Easton owns me!" she cried even louder, her eyes hazy, her lips swollen, and her pussy clenching around my fingers. "Charlie Easton owns my pussy, my body, my mind." Her toes curled. "Me!"

"Good girl," I murmured, kissing on her neck. "That's my good fucking girl."

CHAPTER
THIRTY-EIGHT

ATHENA

ONCE WE RETURNED FROM RADIANT, showered, and changed into comfy pajamas, I grabbed one of the candles that I had made a couple of weeks ago with Charlie's favorite scent—strawberry—and headed to the living room.

Charlie cut a slice of cheesecake for us in the kitchen, staying silent.

The silence was almost eerie because, usually, Charlie was wound up with excitement and confidence. It was rare that I saw him look so … gloomy, especially after we had just come home from an activity that he'd planned.

"What's wrong?" I asked as he approached.

"Nothing."

I lit the candle and watched him place down the plate on the table. Something was wrong.

Maybe he was coming down from the high of being at Radiant together. Maybe he needed something that the girls called aftercare. Heather and Sierra always talked about it, but never really explained what it was.

So, I sat down on the couch and tugged on his shoulder. "Come here."

Charlie moved closer to me and laid his head on my lap. I drew my fingers through his white-blonde hair and massaged his scalp. He closed his eyes and finally relaxed for the first time since we made it home.

"Are you okay?" I asked.

"Yes."

"You know that you can tell me."

"I know."

Silence followed, and when I didn't think that he would open up to me tonight, I grabbed the plate of cheesecake from Dough-burgh and broke a piece off with my fork, feeding it to Charlie, who happily accepted.

I took a piece for myself and stared out our window and into the city. It was so beautiful, even in the freezing cold, even in the dead of winter. The city lights always made me happy. It was one of the reasons Charlie had picked this apartment for us.

Charlie shifted in my arms, and I returned my attention to him.

When I went out with the girls, they always talked about aftercare. I always thought it was weird because their sex lives were amazing, but they'd talk about how they loved aftercare so much more …

Now, I finally understood it.

I closed my eyes and drew my finger through his hair. This was more than nice. This was the calm *after* the storm—quiet and intimate, peaceful and relaxing after being worked up for hours at Radiant.

"I love you, Charlie Easton," I murmured to him. "That's never going to change."

Again, more silence, but this time, his entire body became tense. So, I opened my eyes and gazed down at him, gently tilting his face up at me. There were tears in his eyes, and he was biting down on his bottom lip, the way he did whenever he was upset.

"Do you promise?" he whispered.

My eyes widened, tears welling in them. Charlie Easton never cried in front of me. Ever.

Seeing him so distraught, seeing him this upset, killed me on the inside.

I pulled him tighter. "I promise, Charlie. I will always love you, no matter what."

He buried his face into my lap, his shoulders jerking slightly as he let out a muffled whimper. I rubbed his back, a few tears slipping down my cheeks.

What had Charlie's father said to him at Radiant?

"And if I ... if I don't make it in the business," he asked, "will you still love me?"

"Yes, I'll still love you," I whispered, taking his face in my hands. "Stop it."

He sat and shook his head, staring at me with so much pain on his face. "If I lose you—no, no. I can't lose you. I've waited so long for you to be mine, but I feel like everything is falling out of place. I feel like the whole world is against me, between the fundraising and my father, Derek ..."

I pushed his tears away with my thumbs. This had all come on so suddenly.

"I don't care how much money you make. I don't care if your business succeeds or fails. I don't care what we do together. All I want is for you to be happy, Charlie," I whispered.

He had always told me that he didn't care what people thought, but it seemed like he did a bit more than he had led on.

And it was hard to let go, to truly not care about the opinions of others.

"Look at me," I whispered to him, lifting his chin and kissing him on the lips, tasting the saltiness of his tears. "You're mine as much as I'm yours, and I won't give up on you, no matter what happens between us or to us."

If I had known that the man at brunch was Charlie's father, I never would've said anything to him and really wouldn't have let him pay. I thought it was an innocent interaction, someone finding our girl group cute and wanting to make our day.

After Charlie had told me the truth, I knew his father had done that to make Charlie upset.

"I love you," he whispered against my lips, resting his forehead on mine.

"I love you too, Charlie."

ATHENA

SUN and I flew down the highway in my car on our way to the coffee shop, music blasting so loud that it vibrated the car. I bobbed my head to the rhythm and ignored the cop that we had passed, hoping he wouldn't pull me over.

Man, for the past few days, I'd felt like I was on top of the world.

Moving her head back and forth, Sun hummed and stared out the window. I took the exit for Carnegie and followed the road toward the coffee shop. Outside, a light drizzle of rain pattered against the windshield.

I parked the car, paid the meter on my phone, and grabbed my bag from the trunk.

"I'm so jealous of you and Charlie," Sun hummed. "You guys are perfect together."

Playfully, I rolled my eyes. "Oh, come on …"

"Seriously though," Sun said. "You're so lucky."

"Lucky that I'm married and don't remember the wedding?"

She sighed softly, stepped into the café, and shook off her jacket. "I don't know if I will ever have that with Russ and Maya.

They're really happy together, and I definitely add to the relationship, but ..."

"But what? You're happy with them."

"At some point, I want to get married too. But they've already had a wedding. They are already set into their life. I don't know if they would accept me into their marriage, as more than just a doll they can use."

I frowned when her frown deepened. "Ah, Sun."

Honestly, I wasn't sure what to say or how to even say it. Since the day we had met, Charlie and I had been friends and connected on an emotional level. Sun's relationship was physical, but it definitely had emotional elements to it.

I had seen how Maya looked at her when Sun turned away. I had seen the jealousy in Russ's eyes when someone at Radiant paid a bit too much attention to her the other day. It was more than physical to them.

But was it relationship-worthy? Marriage-worthy? I didn't know.

"You know," I said, curling my arm around hers, "I think they really like you."

"For my body."

Heather and Sierra waved from a table, and I tugged Sun into line to grab tea.

"I mean, of course they like your body," I said, stepping back and checking her out in front of everyone so she knew she looked good. "Look at how sexy you are. Who wouldn't want to—"

Sun waved her hand in the air and shook her head. "Don't be so loud!"

My lips curled into a smirk, and I rocked forward on my heels. "I'm just saying!"

Cheeks flaming red, Sun narrowed her eyes. "We're out in public. Not everyone has to know that I have—"

"A smoking hot boyfriend and an even sexier girlfriend? Because if it were me"—I giggled—"I would want everyone to know how I scored with two scorching hot billionaires who took me on vacations, and let me stay at their place, and took me out on dates, and got jealous when I talked to other people."

"They do not—" Sun started.

"Hey, girls!" the barista said, smiling at us. "What're we having?"

We moved to the counter, and I gazed at all the delicious baked goods they had today. Strawberry cake, scones, brownies, and cookies that had the chocolate chips gooey and melting.

"Just a hot tea," Sun said.

"Me too," I added, handing the barista my card.

After she gave us our drinks, Sun sipped hers. "As I was saying, they do not get jealous."

"Yes, they do."

"No, they don't."

"Yes, they do," Heather called from our table. "They totally do."

I dragged Sun over to them and plopped down next to Heather. "Told you."

Still in denial, Sun shook her head. "They do not. Don't get my hopes up."

"Girl!" Heather said. "If you don't get your head out of the trash can, I'm going to smack you out of there. Literally *every time* any of us sees you with them, they're staring at you so possessively ..." Heather shook. "Gosh, it's so hot."

"That doesn't mean—ow!" Sun exclaimed. "Did you just kick me?!"

Heather raised her brows. "I told you to stop talking bad about yourself."

From across the table, Sierra smirked. "If you don't think they're into you, then you should flirt with someone in front of them to see how they react. Chances are that they'll get possessive enough for you to see it."

Evelyn walked over to the table in a set of heels and pulled up a chair from another table to sit. She placed her coffee on the table and wiggled her brows. "But make sure you do it at Radiant so we can all watch."

Sun scrunched up her nose. "No!"

I snickered and pulled out my textbook to study for the bar. It was approaching quickly.

After the other night, when Charlie had cried in my arms because he didn't think he was good enough, I had decided that I needed to study for the bar every chance that I had. I wanted to pass with flying colors and become a successful lawyer so Charlie didn't have to worry.

I wanted him to work on his business because he loved it.

Not because his parents forced him into it or made him feel like he had to do anything to succeed. I didn't want him to trade in his values for a few extra bucks. We didn't have to be billionaires or even millionaires. As long as we stayed together, I'd be happy.

"That's it," Evelyn said, tugging out her laptop to work. "I'm calling in reinforcements."

"Reinforcements?!" Sun exclaimed. "Gosh, I should've never told you guys."

"All I'm saying is," Evelyn started, "next time you're at Radiant, be prepared."

Sun stared in horror. "Be prepared for what?"

My lips curled into a smirk. "Oh, you know …"

"No, I really don't!"

"To get dicked down by some hottie." Evelyn giggled.

"No!" Sun shouted. "I don't want to get dicked down by anyone except Russ."

Heather wiggled her brows. "That's who she's talking about, especially after Russ and Maya see a sexy older couple talking to you." She giggled behind her hand. "Oh God, this is going to be so good."

CHAPTER
FORTY

CHARLIE

"HEY, CHARLIE!" Winter said at Radiant's coatroom, beaming at me when I walked in for my meeting with Michelle. She had pulled her brown hair into a high ponytail. "Didn't expect to see you here today."

I clenched my jaw. *Damn it, I knew I shouldn't have come here alone.*

But I hadn't wanted to disrupt Athena. I really wanted to make this partnership work because, no matter what Athena said, she deserved it. Athena deserved everything that I could give her and more.

Instead of answering Winter, I placed my coat down on the counter and headed right for Michelle's office in the back hallway with my bag. Winter called after me to make small talk, but I had no drive for small talk with anyone anymore.

Radiant was quiet today, albeit it was early.

Once I made it to Michelle's office, I knocked twice and waited in the hallway. There was some shuffling happening within the room, which sounded like things being knocked over and heels clacking against the ground.

"One sec!" Michelle called.

A moment later, the door opened, and Michelle peered at me, her hair a wild mess and red lipstick—which wasn't her usual color—on her neck. She slipped into the hallway and smoothed out her wrinkled dress.

"Just finishing up in here," Michelle said, wiping some red lipstick off the corner of her lip. "You're here early. Why don't I meet you at the bar in five minutes?"

The door opened behind Michelle, and a pretty woman with dark brown hair and bright red lips scurried out of the room, throwing a wink toward Michelle and running down the hall while trying to tug on her clothes.

When she disappeared, I opened my mouth to say something quirky to Michelle, only for the door to open again. This time, another woman with bright pink lipstick slipped out the door while fastening her bra.

My lips curled into a smirk. "Damn, okay, Michelle."

Michelle rolled her eyes. "What?"

"How many more do you have in there?"

"Oh, shush it, you," she said, playfully pushing me away. "I'll see you in five."

After chuckling, I headed back toward the main area, passed Winter, who giggled and waved while I ignored her, and grabbed a drink at the bar from Abdul. I swished it in my mouth and drank some down.

"You see your dad since the other night?" Abdul asked.

"No, thank God," I mumbled. "But I have to see him this weekend."

My stomach twisted into knots, and I stared emptily at the whiskey in my glass. After swirling it around, I took a sip and placed it down on the bar in front of me. The party was Saturday night, and I had to see those stupid fuckers.

"No offense," he said, "but he's kind of a dick."

"Tell me about it."

Five minutes later, Michelle bounced to the bar with her

makeup freshened up and her hair back to normal, as if what I had caught her doing never happened. She slipped onto a stool next to me. "So, what'd you want to talk about? Business, you said?"

"I've been working on a virtual reality experience for sex workers, porn stars, and people in the industry," I said, opening up my laptop bag and tugging out the small equipment to show her, if she requested it.

"A VR experience?" she hummed. "Sounds fun. So, basically, immersive VR porn."

I half shrugged. "Kinda. You already have an established brand, and a partnership will benefit both of us. Your users receive a new experience, and you can find new and interested members of your company. And I can get this off the ground."

"Stop being so formal with me," she said. "Business is personal. Always."

"Sorry," I said, scratching the back of my head and opening the laptop.

Michelle followed my gaze to my screen, then to the small pieces of equipment in my hands. She called for Abdul to get her favorite drink and leaned forward. "How's Athena feel about this?"

"She's known what it is for a while," I said. "She's fine with it."

Besides, it wasn't like I was going out and fucking women, and neither was she. While I'd still worked in porn, I had hired a few developers to code the project, and I had tested it. It was really, really, really close to becoming fully immersive too.

Not just wearing a bulky headset.

"All right, well, I want to try it," Michelle said. "Where's the headset?"

I placed the small equipment in her hands.

"What's this?" Michelle asked.

"VR," I said. "You attach the dots to your temple."

"Who created it?"

"I did."

"I've never seen anything like this before," she said, placing the dots on her temple. They stuck to her skin, and I loaded the experience on the computer. "Usually, it's a huge headset or glasses. Nothing so … slim and sleek."

"Close your eyes," I said.

She sat back in the seat and closed her eyes for a handful of minutes, and then she tugged the dots off her temples and looked at me through wide eyes. "Charlie, this is the best VR that I've used."

I offered a smile. "Thanks."

"I'm serious," she said, handing me the equipment. "Why are you just using this for porn? You could sell this hardware and software for ten billion dollars to any big company trying to break into the space."

"It's important to me that they allow not-safe-for-work content," I said. "If I sell it to a big company, they'll most likely ban it from any type of adult content. All these companies and banks have a problem with it."

"Who created it?" she asked. "Did you hire someone?"

"Well, sorta," I said. "I created the hardware and the connection to the brain."

"You really created this yourself?" she asked.

"The hardware, yes. But I had the porn experience developed by software engineers."

"Yeah, but *you* created the VR … I can't even call this a headset. You created this?"

It was almost as if she didn't believe it.

"If you really want a partnership, I would love to partner with you," she said, pausing. "But it'd be wrong of me not to push you to launch this yourself. Sure, we can work together to offer this at Radiant and on my site, but you need to get this out to VR gaming companies. You need to find a price point that can be affordable for everyone without breaking the bank. You want to get this in every house in the world. Not just people looking for porn."

"You think so?"

"One hundred percent. Steven has more contacts than me in this space," she said. "You should talk to him."

My lips curled into a smile. "Thank you."

"But"—she grabbed my shoulder—"I still want you to add this product and the software that you created onto my website. If it's fair to you, we can do a fifty-fifty split in royalties for every unit sold. Sound like a deal?"

She held out her hand, and I shook it.

"Deal."

FORTY-ONE

ATHENA

I WALKED out of the bathroom in the dress that I planned to wear to Charlie's family's party tonight.

"Dayum!" Heather shouted in the middle of her and Hector's living room.

They had been doing me up all day, pampering me, along with everything else that best friends did because I ... was nervous as heck.

"You think it looks okay?" I asked, smoothing it out.

"If I were Charlie, I would fuck you so hard," Heather said.

My cheeks flamed, and I shuffled awkwardly into the center of the room. Charlie fucking me really wasn't the goal of this dress, and besides, I didn't want Derek or his father—God forbid—to feel the same way.

Yuck!

I would rather die than let Charlie's father watch us fuck again.

Sierra giggled and playfully shoved Heather. "Seriously, you look so hot!"

Evelyn drew her fingers through my hair to loosen my curls. "They're all going to be so jealous."

"Girl, *I'm* jealous of you!" Heather exclaimed, fanning herself. "The things I would do to—"

"Heather!" I exclaimed. "Save your flirting for when Sun gets here. She loves it."

Sun totally *did not* like the flirting that Heather did with her, but it was funny and cute to see her all flustered. Besides, it only made me more nervous because I did *not* want to look fuckable tonight!

I wanted to be pretty and respectable.

While I was happy that they had confidence that tonight would go well, I did not. My stomach had been twisting into tight knots since I had woken up. Nothing could ever go smoothly, and this wasn't an exception.

"All right, all right," I said, grabbing my coat and shrugging it on. "I need to get back to our place. Charlie is waiting for me, and I still need to pick up some wine to bring to the party. I don't want to go empty-handed."

I wasn't into that rich kinda alcohol, but I definitely needed something.

Once I grabbed all my stuff and endured a couple more flirtatious remarks from Heather, I headed out the door and made a sprint for the elevator before Heather could smack my ass on the way out.

Her giggles echoed down the hall, and I slipped into the elevator and hit the bottom button. When I hit the ground floor, I found my way to my car and began my short drive down to the liquor store.

After parallel parking in these six-inch heels, I hopped onto the sidewalk and headed right for the liquor store. The bell rang when I stepped in, and the man up front smiled at me. I politely smiled back and wandered through the store, phone in hand to text Charlie.

Me: What kind of wine should I grab?

Once I slipped my phone into my pocket, I headed toward the sweet white wine and scanned the aisle for my favorite kind. Who enjoyed that disgusting bitter red wine anyway? Not me. I needed something sugary.

Where is it? Come on. It has to be here somewhere.

On the second-to-top shelf, I spotted my favorite kind and stood on my toes in these heels to reach it without dropping the thing—because my clumsy ass totally would. Once I secured the goods, my phone buzzed.

I tucked my bottle of wine underneath my arm and yanked out the device. It had to be Charlie responding to my message, probably telling me that they didn't deserve any kind of wine because they were dickheads.

But when I looked at my notifications, it was an unknown number with an attachment.

Unknown: Athena, I think you'll want to see this.

I narrowed my eyes at the message and hesitantly clicked on it—because who the hell was it, and what did they want me to see? No way was I clicking on any links, but it wouldn't hurt to look at the attachment. Besides, I needed to click on it to block the number.

The video started playing on the screen, and I quickly realized that it was Charlie tugging off his shirt … in his bedroom … with none other than Nadia on his bed, naked and playing with herself in front of the camera.

CHAPTER
FORTY-TWO

ATHENA

NO. *No, this has to be … this can't be real. It's* not *real.*

Tears pricked the corners of my eyes, and I shook my head. Charlie wouldn't do this to me. Charlie loved me. Charlie only wanted me. He wouldn't betray me like this. He'd promised to love me forever.

But … it looked just like him.

Him and Nadia? Really?

I needed to get out of here. Now.

My legs moved toward the front, and I placed the wine on the counter, biting back a sob. My chest moved up and down quickly, heart racing faster than it ever had. My throat felt like it was closing up … like …

"Ma'am? Your license?" the cashier asked.

I snapped my gaze up to him, barely able to see him through my teary eyes, and fished my wallet out of my purse. With shaky hands, I grabbed my license and handed it to him.

When did this happen? Maybe before we got together?

Yeah, that has to be it, right? Maybe they made a film before we got together.

The cashier handed me back my license. "That'll be twenty-nine dollars and ninety-nine cents."

After fumbling with the license, I gave the man my card and kept my head down. He swiped it and handed it back to me, bagging up my wine. My eyes burned with salty tears, and I quickly pushed a stray one off my cheek.

"Here you go."

Once I grabbed my wine, I hurried out of the liquor store and toward my car down the street. The harsh wind did nothing to help me right now. I kept my gaze focused on the ground and then closed my eyes.

"Fuck," I whispered. "Fuck!"

When I reopened my eyes, I had no time to stop myself before I slammed right into someone. He wrapped his hands around my elbows to stop me from falling backward, then steadied me.

"Athena," he murmured. "What are you doing out here? Alone? Crying?"

I looked up and locked eyes with the one and only Derek Easton.

As soon as my gaze landed on Derek, I snapped back to my senses. It wasn't Charlie in that video; it was Derek, trying to frame Charlie. It was Derek, trying to make me a mess of emotions. It was Derek, about to try to take advantage of the situation.

"I'm fine," I whispered, wiping away my tears and stumbling back in my heels.

Derek stepped closer. "You're crying."

I moved back again, but my heel got caught on an uneven piece of sidewalk, and I tripped backward onto my ass. Derek did nothing to stop me this time as he stepped closer to me until he was at my feet.

My hands stung. They had to be scraped from the fall.

"Stay away from me," I whispered.

A low chuckle left his mouth, and then he became quiet. "No."

Before I could stop him, he scooped me up and slapped a hand over my mouth. I screamed into it, biting down on the skin and tasting blood, but he didn't even react. I kicked and elbowed and punched, doing whatever the hell I could do to get out of the situation.

The more I struggled, the tighter his hold on me became.

One second, he was strutting down the sidewalk with me, and the next, he was throwing me into the trunk of his car. My dress was torn and dirty with brown slush, my hands covered in blood. I landed with a thud.

Almost immediately, I tried to scramble out of the trunk so he couldn't close it on me. But it suddenly came down hard on my head, knocking me back. My head bounced against the bottom of the trunk, my vision blurring.

The trunk opened again, and I thought I could escape. So, I used all my strength and pushed myself forward toward the light. But the trunk came down on me again, hitting my head, my fingers getting caught.

I hissed in pain and yanked my fingers back, curling up in the back of the trunk and staring up at the darkness. Stars danced in my vision, and my eyes felt heavy. So heavy. They closed on their own.

I tried to open them back up, but I couldn't. All I could think was that I was going to die.

Derek Easton, the sadistic asshole, was going to kill me.

FORTY-THREE

CHARLIE

I PACED AROUND our living room and peered at my phone again. It had been nearly a half hour since Athena had messaged me about the wine, but I hadn't received a response that she had gotten it and was on her way home.

Hell, it didn't even look like she had read it.

Athie usually read my messages immediately, and she always responded.

My stomach twisted into knots, and I swallowed hard. We should've left for the party ten minutes ago. While I was fine with not going at all, Athie didn't like being late. She wouldn't have gone anywhere else, would she?

When another minute passed and she still hadn't walked through the front door to our apartment, I picked up my phone and called Heather. Athena had gone over to Heather's place this morning to get ready.

The phone rang and rang and rang, then eventually went to voicemail.

"Fuck," I growled, then called Sierra.

It rang twice, and then she answered. "Hello?"

Loud music played in the background. She must be at Radiant. Was Athena there with her? Maybe they had decided to get a drink to calm Athena's nerves before the party. Honestly, I wanted to believe anything at the moment.

But ... I knew something was wrong.

"Sierra, is Athena with you?" I asked.

"What?" she asked. "Hold on. Let me go into the hallway, where it's quieter."

My heart pounded against my rib cage so loudly that I could hear it in my ears. *Fuck.*

A couple of moments later, she returned. "Hey, what's up, Charlie?"

"Is Athena with you?"

"No, she left Heather's place, like, an hour and a half ago," she said. "We're at Radiant."

"Fuck," I whispered, pacing around and running a hand through my hair. "Fuck!"

"Why? She never came home?" Sierra asked, worried.

"No."

"Okay, um, let me see if any of the girls have seen or heard from her," Sierra said, the music becoming louder again. She shouted over the music, then muttered, "I'll call you right back." Then the call ended.

"Fuck!" I shouted, dialing Athena's phone.

Nothing.

I messaged her every way that I could, called her again and again.

Nothing. Nothing. Nothing. Nothing. Nothing!

Deciding that I needed to *find* her, that I could at least search for her car, I grabbed my jacket and threw it over my shoulder. She had been coming home from Heather's house. I knew the route she took. Her car had to be at one of the three liquor stores along the way.

After running to my car, I started it and pressed on the gas, not caring how fast that I went. I needed to find Athena now.

The sooner, the better. Then we wouldn't even go to that stupid fucking party tonight.

We'd go home and forget about it all.

Halfway to the first liquor store, my phone buzzed. Hector.

"None of the girls have seen her," Hector said over the phone. "They're driving around now to all the spots that they hang out at to see if she's there. Sierra said that her phone shows that her last location was at Fifth Avenue, downtown. But that was over thirty minutes ago."

"Fuck," I murmured, running another hand through my hair.

"Steven and I are close," Hector said. "We'll go check it out."

"I'll be there in five minutes."

I drove by the first liquor store, not spotting Athena inside or her car around, so I drove to the next one on Fifth, where Athena's phone had apparently last updated. My heart pounded hard inside my chest, and I swallowed.

Something wasn't right. She wasn't here. I already knew it.

My stomach dropped when I spotted Hector and Steven on the sidewalk in front of Athena's car. But Athena wasn't in it, nor was she with them, nor was she inside the liquor store from what I could tell.

Once I illegally parked in the bus lane, I hopped out of my car and jogged to Hector and Steven, who talked tensely with each other. When I approached, they immediately looked up at me.

"Did you find her?"

"No," I said, looking into her car. "She's not here?"

Hector and Steven shared a look, and then Hector peered down at the sidewalk, where there were a couple of drops of blood. Nothing too suspicious, but ... I knew, deep down, that the blood was from Athena.

Not only that, but there was a diamond on the ground beside it.

The diamond from the ring I'd bought her.

I picked it up, heart racing so loudly that I almost didn't

notice the bus whizzing by and the driver giving me the finger for parking in its lane. My mouth dried.

No. No, I didn't believe it. I didn't want to believe it.

Athena wouldn't … Athena couldn't …

My phone buzzed inside my suit pants, and I yanked it out, answering the call without looking at the contact. It had to be Sierra or Heather, or maybe it was even Athena, calling me back.

"Did you find her?" I asked.

"Find who?" an amused Derek asked over the phone. "Your wife? She's with me."

Adrenaline rushed through me. "What the fuck did you do to her?"

"Say hi, Athie," Derek taunted.

There was silence on the other end, and then my phone buzzed in my hand. I peeled it away from my ear and stared at the pictures on the screen. Rage bubbled up inside me, and I slammed my fist right into Athena's car door.

With blood dripping from a gash in her forehead, Athena lay in a cage in the middle of my parents' living room, naked and on display for my entire family of fucked-up animals.

"Looks like she hasn't woken up yet," Derek hummed. "But don't worry. We'll make sure she gets a good introduction to the family when she does. See you soon, *brother*."

CHAPTER
FORTY-FOUR

ATHENA

HEAD THROBBING, I pressed my hand against it and whimpered. *What happened?*

My body was cold … extremely cold, the ground underneath me like ice. I turned onto my side and curled up into a ball, not wanting to open my eyes.

Last thing I remember was …

What was it again?

I had been at Heather's to get ready for the party, and then I bought wine and saw that video and—

My heart began thumping so loudly that I could hear it in my ears.

And the last thing I remembered was Derek standing over me.

Oh my God.

After willing myself to open my eyes, I tried to adjust to the sudden rush of sensations. There were bright lights pointed on me from all directions, and beyond that, there were people in the darkness.

Faceless men and women. Laughing, drinking, and …

fucking.

"Oh my fucking God," I whispered to myself, eyes widening.

Using all my strength, I pushed myself up to a semi-seated position, resting all my weight on my left arm. Moans drifted out from all places. I spotted glimpses of fur and lace and mesh, ropes and swings.

This can't be happening. This really, really can't be happening.

This wasn't any party. No, this was a sex party.

And Derek had brought me to a sex party? What kind of sick family were the Eastons?! Had Charlie grown up around this? Why hadn't he told me? No, surely, if he had known, then he wouldn't have decided to come here at all. They must've been planning this for a long time now.

Another cold gust of air hit me, and I looked down to see that I wasn't just at a sex party. I was sitting in a cage, naked, at a sex party, in the center of the room, as if I were entertainment. Or maybe ... Derek planned to use me as the main event.

Maybe Charlie's father did.

God, at this point, I wouldn't be surprised if Charlie's mother did too.

"She is finally awake," someone shouted from across the room, which was large enough to be a ballroom.

The crowd parted and quieted like we were in some sort of sick movie, and Derek Easton walked toward me with a smirk stretched across his face.

No. No. No. No. No. No. No.

I scrambled to the back of the cage to keep my distance as he approached.

No. He's going to ... he's planning to ...

Derek pulled off the key around his neck and pushed it into the lock on the cage, opening it up enough to step inside it with me. He closed it behind him, the bright lights bouncing off his dark, sinister features.

He grabbed my ankle and pulled me toward him. I kicked at

him, but it was no use. He easily flipped me around and dropped me on my stomach.

"Charlie!" I screamed at the top of my lungs. "Charlie, please help me!"

"Charlie isn't going to save you this time," Derek murmured into my ear from behind. "Why? Because you're mine. Every woman he's ever been with has become mine, one way or another. You just had to be difficult."

"Get off me," I cried, slamming my shoulder into his chin.

"A difficult bitch," he spit, taking a fistful of my hair and shoving my head down against the bottom of the cage. With his other hand, he grabbed at my hip and pulled them up into the air. "One who will learn how to behave."

Tears pricked the corners of my eyes, but that was exactly what Derek wanted. So, I made sure that none of them fell. I made sure that he didn't have the satisfaction of seeing me cry because of what he planned to do to me.

Instead, I closed my eyes and prepared myself to deal with all the emotional damage that this would bring. I pretended that it was Charlie behind me and not Derek, that the people watching were those from Radiant.

It was the only way that I was going to get through this. I had to believe that Charlie had figured out what had happened to me, that he was doing everything in his power to save me, even if he didn't make it in time.

"Don't have nothing to say now?" Derek growled into my ear from behind, his hand moving across my ass. He smacked it hard enough to definitely leave a bright red handprint. "Hmm?"

I bit back a whimper. "Anything," I corrected.

"What?"

"It's, *Don't have anything to say now?* Not *nothing* to say."

Derek smacked me hard across the cheek—hard enough that I saw stars in my vision. Then he grabbed my hips and lined up right behind me. "I'm going to fuck the bitch right out of you,

Athie. If you're not going to cry, I want to see the tears fall from my brother's eyes."

CHAPTER
FORTY-FIVE

CHARLIE

WHEN I REACHED MY PARENTS' property, the gates were closed.

"We can't let you through," the guard said. "You're not on the guest list."

After throwing the car into park, I leaped out and socked him so hard in the jaw that he collapsed onto the ground. With one arm protecting his face, he grunted and tried to stand, using his other. I grabbed him by the collar, lifted him a few inches into the air, and punched him until his body went limp.

Once he dropped to the ground, I jogged to the security booth, pushed the button to open the gates, and hopped back into my car. I swore to fucking God that I'd torture them—*no, kill them*—if they'd touched Athena.

If one fucking hair on her head was yanked out, I'd lose it.

I pressed my foot all the way down and sped up the driveway. Cars were lined up almost toward the bottom. I sped past everyone and peered into the rearview mirror to see Heather and the other girls behind me, almost as pissed as I was.

When I reached the front entrance, where there was even more security, I hopped out of my car and shoved past them as best as I could. Heather hollered behind me, and a few women screamed, which could only mean that Heather probably had a weapon.

I didn't know—or care—what it was, as long as we got Athena out of here now.

Music thumped through the house, and when I entered, everything was so dark. The overwhelming scent of perfume, cologne, and alcohol drifted through my nose. People were kissing and getting off on each other.

If I had known this was a sex party, I would've never come.

If I had known my parents were into this, I would've cut contact years ago.

If I had thought Athie would be in this much danger, I would've never left her side.

But I knew better now. I fucking knew better.

Scanning the crowd, I spotted the one area in the center that was brightly lit so the entire room could see. A metal cage big enough to fit multiple people inside. A metal cage that housed Athena and Derek.

Athena sat on her hands and knees in the cage, completely naked. Her gaze was cast on the ground, her face scrunched up, and her smaller hands were balled into fists. Derek knelt behind her, with his shit-eating grin.

As if she knew exactly where I was, she snapped her gaze up and locked on to mine.

Rage took over my entire body. I shoved my relatives out of the way, pushed billionaires that my father worked with to the ground, elbowed their wives so they'd move because I needed to save her.

Derek hadn't shoved himself into her yet, though he might have already scarred her.

My legs moved faster than I'd thought possible. Just as Derek slid into Athena and she let out a piercing cry that would haunt me for the rest of eternity, I snapped open the cage door, grabbed him by the neck, and yanked him out.

I slammed him down onto the ground and hurled fists into his face, my entire body trembling with rage and adrenaline. Fist after fist after fist. My vision and memories blacked out. But I kept raining fists, colliding with his face every time.

Before I could land another punch, someone swung a large and thick wooden beam.

"Go get your girl," Heather said to me, slamming the wood into Derek's face again and breaking his nose. "Nobody touches Athena!"

My hands were covered in blood, and I stood up and shuffled back to make sure that Derek wasn't getting back up. When he flinched on the ground, I raced back to Athie, who was curled up in the corner of the cage, weeping silently.

How could I have let this happen? Why hadn't I called her a few minutes earlier? I should've done something. Anything.

Pain squeezed at my chest. I scooped her up into my arms and pulled her to my chest.

For the rest of my life, I wouldn't let myself live this down. My job as Athena's husband was to protect her, and I couldn't even do that. I should've put my foot down when my father asked me to come to the party. I should've killed Derek that night so many weeks ago.

This was my fault. All my fault.

But at least Athena was safe now.

CHAPTER
FORTY-SIX

CHARLIE HELD me tightly and pushed through the crowd that had just watched Derek touch me. A crowd that had done absolutely nothing to stop it. A crowd that had gotten off on my pain, on Derek's superiority over me.

"I'm sorry," Charlie whispered, holding me tightly. "I'm sorry. I'm sorry. I'm so sorry."

But I could barely hear him over Heather shouting like a maniac. She had a wooden beam in her grasp and repeatedly slammed it against Derek's face, which had already been bashed in over and over again.

Hector was behind her, trying to grasp her arm, along with Steven. I spotted my other friends shouting at a couple other people at the party and even spotted a flash of a couple of police officers in the crowd, attempting to control everyone.

I squeezed my eyes closed and prayed to a god I didn't believe in to disappear.

Everyone was staring at me. Everyone had seen what happened.

Suddenly, someone placed a jacket over my naked body in

Charlie's arms. I opened my eyes to see Sun beside me, tugging off her scarf to help cover more of my body. Her friends, Russ and Maya, offered up their coats as well.

I had tried to be strong, but I couldn't help the sob that left my mouth when I saw Charlie. Derek hadn't slammed himself into me at all, but he had been so close that I swore Charlie thought he had.

But I ... I just felt so guilty.

While I had known it was coming, while I expected it, while I *prepared* for it, I felt so disgusting. I didn't want him to touch me, but I'd let it happen.

I wouldn't be surprised if Charlie never wanted to look at me again.

I held my breath, sank into Charlie's hug to steal his warmth, and tried to hold in all the pain. My emotions were a mess right now. I didn't know whether to cry or throw a fit, to march back into the party and kick Derek's ass myself or head back home with Charlie and never leave the house.

Charlie walked with me out of the mansion and to his car, which had almost plowed right into the front entrance. After opening up the back door, he scooted into the seat with me and pressed his lips to my forehead.

"How are you doing?" Sun whispered, sitting on the edge of the seat and rubbing my leg.

I sniffled in response and stared at my best friend through teary eyes. I knew if I opened my mouth, nothing but a sob would escape past my lips. Charlie's family members were still around, and I didn't want them to see me like this.

"Please take me home," I finally whimpered into his shoulder, clutching on to his back like if I let go, then it would be the actual death of me. Like if I released my grip, then Derek would seize my hips and pull me back to him. "I never wanna come back here again."

Charlie kissed my forehead. "We are *never* coming back here again."

"I'll drive you both to the hospital," Sun said to Charlie. "You stay back there with her."

"I don't want to go to the hospital," I whimpered. "I want to go home."

"You have to go to the hospital," Sun said. "Your head is bleeding profusely."

"You need to be checked out," Charlie agreed.

After I pressed my trembling lips together, Sun drove off the property and onto the road.

I let out a low breath, almost a sigh of relief. I couldn't believe that this had happened. I couldn't believe that … that Derek really was almost … inside me.

I intertwined my shaky hands to steady them and immediately noticed that …

Wait, where's my diamond?

The ring was still on my finger, but the diamond … it wasn't in its place anymore. It wasn't …

"Charlie," I whispered, tears beginning to pour down my face, "I don't know where my diamond went. I … it must've fallen off when I fell back in the city. I promise … I promise that I didn't do it purposefully. I'm sorry. I'm so sorry."

"Shh, shh, shh," Charlie murmured, hugging me tighter. "It's okay."

"No, it's not okay. I lost my ring, and Derek … and Derek …"

"Calm down, Athena," Charlie whispered against my forehead. "You should be resting. It's okay. I found the diamond, and even if I hadn't, we could replace it. I can't fucking replace you. I need you to be okay."

My eyes burned, and I bit back a sob because it felt so stupid to cry. "I …"

Charlie grasped my face and pulled back so I looked directly into his eyes. "I love you."

The whimper slipped past my quivering lips. "I love you too. So much. I'm sor—"

"Stop it," Charlie said. "You've done nothing wrong."

"If I were you, I wouldn't touch me," I said truthfully. "Derek touched me."

At the mention of his brother, Charlie gritted his teeth, his gaze distancing. Sun looked back at us through the mirror and grimaced, her hands tightening on the steering wheel. Charlie shook his head.

"Don't say shit like that, Athena," he murmured. "I love you, no matter what. No matter what happened to you, to me, to *us*, I will love you, even after I take my last breath."

CHAPTER
FORTY-SEVEN

ATHENA

"YOU NEED TO REST," Sun said, ushering me to my bedroom. "No watching movies."

I stared over my shoulder and into the living room, but Charlie stepped into my line of sight, following close behind us. He pulled down the blankets on my bed and gathered some pillows for me.

"But I really want to watch. We were sitting in the hospital for over two hours."

And honestly, I wanted to get my mind off everything that had happened tonight.

Sitting at the hospital … all I could do was think about Derek's hands all over me. Every time that Charlie had looked my way, I felt so … guilty. I didn't mean to, and I knew he hadn't seen it that way either. But still …

"You need to rest," Charlie said, agreeing with Sun.

After pouting, I slipped into my bed and rested my head against the propped-up pillows. I closed my eyes and blew out a deep breath, remembering Charlie's horrific expression when he had seen me in that cage.

"Do you still love me?" I whispered, though I knew he did. I just needed reassurance.

"Yes," he said, sliding into the bed with me, one arm around my waist.

"Promise?"

"I promise."

Sun shuffled out of the room. "I'll get you some water."

A couple of moments later, I listened to the front door open, and two more sets of feet scurried around our apartment. Sun returned with a glass of water and with Sierra and Evelyn, both pale with worried expressions.

"How are you feeling?" Sierra asked.

"Not good," I whispered, clutching my head. "My head is killing me."

"Don't touch your bandages!" Sun exclaimed, shaking her head. She set the glass of water down and clicked her tongue at me. "You've been picking at them since we left the hospital, and you don't want your head to get infected."

"It won't get infected."

"You don't know that." Sun pointed a finger at Charlie. "You'd better make sure she doesn't touch them when I'm gone. You know how she is."

"Maybe Doughburgh could cheer you up?" Evelyn said, handing me a bag of sweets.

I peered into the paper bag and spotted a sampling of almost everything that they had. Warmth drifted through my body, and I held the bag to my chest, lips quivering. No, Doughburgh couldn't make up for what had just happened. But my best friends sure did try.

"Thank you." I glanced at the door, waiting for Heather to barge in. "Where's Heather?"

The girls looked at each other.

"Heather is ..." Sun started.

Evelyn scratched her head. "You know, she's ..."

"Heather said that she hopes you're okay," Sierra said,

chewing on her inner cheek. "She kinda maybe got arrested for beating Derek up with the intent to kill him, and Hector's trying to bail her out now."

While that was serious, a laugh left my mouth.

"Only Heather …" I murmured, closing my eyes and resting my head against Charlie's.

After a few seconds, silence filled the room, and my eyes became heavy. Maybe Sun was right. I did need some rest after what had happened today. The past twelve hours felt like an eternity.

"We'll let you rest," Sun said. "Call us if you need anything."

"Okay," I whispered, watching as they headed into the hallway.

"Hey, you guys," I called. When they turned around, my lips quivered. "Thank you."

FORTY-EIGHT

CHARLIE

"YOU'RE GOING to do great today, baby," I said, kissing just below Athena's bandages on her forehead as I dropped her off at her test-taking facility so she could do the bar exam.

She had been studying nonstop for the past two weeks since the incident.

"I hope so," she whispered, clutching her stomach. "I'm nervous."

I intertwined our fingers and squeezed, walking her to the door. "Don't be nervous."

She stopped on the stairway. "What if I don't pass?"

"Then you can take it again in six months," I said. "But you'll pass. You've studied."

Honestly, I believed that she had been studying so much to get her mind off what had happened. I wasn't quite sure that she had processed any part of the incident fully yet, or maybe not at all. She didn't talk about it, and I wasn't sure if I should bring it up.

All I wanted was for her to be okay.

Maybe after the exam, she'd go to therapy, or at least talk it out.

After chewing on the inside of her cheek, she placed a kiss on my lips. "Thank you."

"I'll be here to pick you up in a couple of hours," I said.

When she disappeared through the building doors, I slumped my shoulders forward. I really hoped that she passed. I think she would, but I was afraid that if she didn't, then everything would hit her at once.

My phone buzzed in my pocket.

Steven: We still on for coffee in ten?

Me: Yes. Be there soon.

I swung my keys around my finger and headed back to my car. Steven and I had officially teamed up on the project, and today was the first day that we were sitting down to review a business plan.

When I reached the car, my phone buzzed again.

Heather: Look at this. =D

A moment later, an image of Derek popped up on the screen. Not only were there still huge gashes in his face, but his nose was broken in three places, and his forehead caved inward from Heather's bashes.

Heather: Apparently, he wants plastic surgery to repair his face.

Heather: Good luck getting that in prison, asshole!

Thankfully, Heather hadn't gotten into much trouble with the police after smashing Derek's face in, but we had pressed charges on Derek for kidnapping and sexually assaulting Athena. He had been taken into the station immediately after we brought Athena home.

My family had tried to pay their way out of it, but there was clear video evidence of him smashing Athena's head with the car trunk. I had hurled more than once while watching it and wanted to wrap my hands around his throat and kill him myself.

But that would mean *I'd* go to jail, and Athena would be all alone.

Not going to fucking happen.

Me: Everything that he got was well deserved.

Athena wasn't in danger from him any longer, though I still worried about what my father might try to do. To combat that, we were officially moving. I didn't know where yet, somewhere in Pittsburgh, but he wouldn't have our address any longer.

I was going to do everything in my power to keep my girl safe. Forever.

CHAPTER
FORTY-NINE

ATHENA

I STARED down at my ring, which Charlie had fixed for me last week.

I honestly didn't know how I was doing on the exam. It was two days of nonstop questions, and I really couldn't focus. My mind wandered to Derek so many times and everything that had happened the past few weeks. I hated that he was in my head now. I hated that the thought of him, that his fingers, were burned into my memory forever.

Charlie didn't deserve that, and I was trying hard to get over it.

And maybe he was right. Maybe I needed therapy.

No, I definitely need therapy.

I just didn't want to go. I hadn't had time to go, up until now. It would take at least ten weeks for the results for the exams to come back.

But did I want to go? No. I didn't want to go. I didn't want to relive it over and over and over again. I didn't want to have nightmares of him. He was in jail now, but I was sure he would get out. At least with all the money his family had.

And what would happen to Charlie's father? Would he find me again too? What were his plans with me? Because I knew it didn't stop at Derek.

I chewed on the inside of my cheek and reviewed my answers for today's exam. Who knew if I had gotten anything right? I could barely remember studying the past few weeks, but I knew what I had done to throw myself away from all the heartache.

After sighing, I blew out another low, long breath and stood up to submit my exam. I hated this. I didn't know if I would pass. I didn't know if I'd become a lawyer, which was all I'd ever wanted to be.

Tears welled in my eyes, and I drew my thumb across my ring again. Charlie flashed in my mind, and I knew I had to do this. I had tried my hardest.

So, after submitting my exam, I gathered my belongings and walked out of the room. The hallway was long and cold and deserted, just like my thoughts. When I reached the exit door, I sighed again and pushed it open.

Charlie stood next to his car on the street, leaning against it and smiling at me. When I saw him, warmth gathered in my chest. I didn't know how he did it, but I just became happy again with him.

He had always had that thing about him. I always, you know, forgot about all my problems when I was with him. Since the day I'd met him, I had known he would be in my life forever.

I descended the stairs and jogged to him. He opened his arms and enveloped me into a hug, stuffing his face into the crook of my neck and kissing just below my ear.

"How did you do?" he asked, beaming with excitement.

I pulled away. My fingers curled into his hair and stared up at him. "I'm not sure how I did. I hope I did good and ..." My heart pounded inside my chest, so loudly that I could hear it in my ears. I didn't want to admit it, but I knew I had to.

"And what?"

I chewed on the inside of my cheek again, tearing off more skin and almost bleeding. "And I think I'm ready for therapy."

"Therapy? I'd be happy to bring you there. Do you want me to come with you?"

"No, not right now. I think I need to go by myself first. Just for a little bit."

"Okay," he said, planting another kiss on my neck. "That's fine with me, but first, we need to celebrate."

"There's nothing to celebrate yet," I said. "I'm not sure if I passed."

"There's so much to celebrate! What are you talking about? You finished the bar! I think that calls for Doughburgh. Don't you think?"

My lips turned up into a small smile, and I felt a giggle bubble in my chest. "Yeah. Actually ... that sounds great. Let's go!"

To continue Athena and Charlie's story in their double epilogue, click here.

ALSO BY EMILIA ROSE

Stepbrother

Poison

The Bad Boy

Detention

My Brother's Best Friend

Science Project

Excite Me

Mafia Boss

Mafia Toy

Mafia Betrayal

Sex Education

Bound By My Father's Best Friend

Pornstar

Submitting to the Alpha

Come Here, Kitten

My Werewolf Professor

The Twins

Four Masked Wolves

Monster Lover

My Bad Boy Alpha

Alpha Maddox

Summoning Sex Demons

The Breeding Cave

Next Door Incubus

ABOUT THE AUTHOR

Emilia Rose is a USA Today bestselling author of steamy romance. She loves writing about dirty-talking bad boys who are obsessed with innocent, and sometimes insecure, virgin heroines. She currently lives in a small town in Connecticut USA with her husband and three playful cats.

Join Emilia's newsletter for exclusive giveaways, early chapter releases, and more!